Drake

The Powers That Be
Book 5

Harper Bentley

Check out other titles by Harper Bentley:

The Powers That Be series:

Gable (The Powers That Be Book 1)

Zeke (The Powers That Be Book 2)

Loch (The Powers That Be Book 3)

Ryker (The Powers That Be Book 4)

CEP series:

Being Chased (CEP #1)

Unbreakable Hearts (CEP #2)

Under the Gun (CEP #3)

The High Rise series

The Fighter

Serenity Point series:

Bigger Than the Sky (Serenity Point Book 1)

Always and Forever (Serenity Point Book 2)

True Love series:

Discovering Us (True Love #1)

Finding Us (True Love #2)

Finally Us (True Love Book 3)

True Love: The Trilogy: The Complete Boxed Set

The Wait series:

Thursdays (The Wait Book 1)

http://harperbentleywrites.com/

Dedication

To my family

Who've been nothing but supportive

from day one

I love you all

♥

ACKNOWLEDGMENTS

To Renee whose encouragement, love and steady guidance for, oh, like, my entire life has made all the difference. I love you soooooo much and can't wait for you to join me in this craziness! Mwah! ♥

To Franca, Mel & Sam, You guys. I know I thank you every time but, my lord, I mean it every single time too. You guys are the best of the best of the best! Thank you for always being there for me! It makes my heart so happy to know that I can text/message/email and you all are there in a flash. I love you all TONS!

To the Harlots & Hellbenders, Oh, how you lovelies never cease to amaze me! To Shannon, Michelle, Gemma & Swess especially, thank you for your endless support & promoting my books! You guys all rock my friggin' world! <3 you hard!

Anne Mercier, Your friendship means the world to me! You are the most generous and sweetest person ever! Knowing I can text/message/call/send smoke signals at any time & you're there no matter what makes me flove you even more. Cage match 2017 fast approaching! Can't wait to give you a big ol' slobbery cheek smooch & great big bearhug! Love you much! xo

TC Matson, Well, damn. Look at all the shit we've been through over the past 2 ½ years and yet we're still acknowledging each other's existence lmao! I lobe you gobs & appreciate everything from the quick text messages cheering me on to the 2-hour phone calls where we scheme to take over the world. One day, drinks are on me, baby hands ;)

To Amy Dunlap, who I forgot to mention in my last book & I'm truly sorry. Your loads of encouragement & love for my books astounds me. You're truly a sister to me which is crazy! Miss you & love you bunches! <3

Erin Spencer, Thank you for always hooking me up at the last minute. I'm thinking you're starting to figure out my MO now so I'm past the shocking you stage. <3 you more!

To the many bloggers who've spread the word about my books, thank you x a kajillion. Know that you are appreciated GOBS!

And to the readers, this is all for you. Thank you for making my dreams come true <3

CHAPTER 1

"Victor! Betsy won't start again," I said to my brother from where I stood in his bedroom door.

His flavor-of-the-day turned over in bed, squinting at me through a tangle of bleached-blond hair. As she shifted, I got a glimpse of naked body parts that I never wanted to see, not in a million-bazillion years, and looked quickly away. Gross.

"Hey," she mumbled, putting her arm out and shaking my brother by the shoulder. "Some whiny chick in scrubs wants you."

I rolled my eyes at her wanting to tell her to fuck off, but odds were I'd never see her again. So instead of wasting my breath, I put her on ignore and crossing my arms on my chest called, "Vic!"

"What?" came his muffled reply from under his pillow.

"My truck won't start," I repeated, wondering if maybe good old Betsy had finally bitten the dust for good.

"Get the screwdriver. Put it in the choke on the carburetor. It'll start," he grumbled.

On a sigh, I answered, "I tried that. It didn't work. Can you give me a lift?"

"Call Jeremiah," he mumbled.

Jeremiah was my "kind of" boyfriend of almost four months. "He's working."

"Jesus," I heard Victor groan, then a moment later his pillow flew across the room and with a kick of his legs he sat up in bed.

Before I saw anything naked on *him* I didn't want to see, I scooted out of his room hollering, "I'll be in the kitchen waiting!"

I felt bad asking him to take me because he was a bartender/assistant manager at a fairly upscale and popular bar and usually didn't get home until around four in the morning. And after calculating in time for his banging this latest chick—again, gross—he'd probably only gotten a couple hours of sleep. Oh, well. But no way was I going to pay a cab to take me to class.

Now glancing at the clock on the stovetop, I saw that if I held my mouth just right—and he got up instead of canoodling some more with the chick in his bed—I'd barely make it to class on time. That was a big, fat if, especially if the chippy he'd brought home had been any good. Annnnd even grosser.

But lo and behold, I heard the bathroom door close and quietly rejoiced that he'd gotten up.

A few minutes later, I heard the sharp *click! click! click!* of heels on the hardwood floor and Vic's one-nighter rounded the corner and entered the kitchen. She stopped, giving me a once-over, eyebrows raised, showing she wasn't one-bit impressed with my purple scrubs. I raised my eyebrows right back, taking in the silver micro-mini dress she wore under a white faux-fur coat and stifled a laugh.

Would these chicks never learn that that shit might get Vic for one night but that was about it?

"I'm Cheri. Victor's girlfriend," she challenged, cocking a hip and putting her hand on it, striking a pose like she was a model who'd stopped at the end of the runway before making the turn.

"I'm Honor. Victor's sister," I revealed, watching her attitude dissolve right in front of my eyes at finding out I wasn't the competition.

"Oh! Nice to meet you!" she replied, all grins and cheery now.

Uh huh. Sure.

"Likewise," I murmured just as Vic came in wearing his usual jeans and long-sleeved thermal.

"Ready?" he asked, looking at me and running a hand over his buzz cut. He grabbed his black leather jacket off the hook by the back door and pulled it on.

"Yep," I answered, peering at the clock again knowing I'd *just* make it on time if he sped a little, which I was certain he would.

"Oh! I'll leave my number," the blonde said. She wrote it out in pink chalk on the board I'd hung next to the back door and turning to Victor suggested, "Walk me out?"

His eyes cut to mine. "Meet you at the bike," he stated then followed her out the door.

Just as I was thinking that at least he was being a gentleman, as he went by, he reached a hand out to the board and smeared her number leaving it illegible. Jeez. My brother the player. I shook my head and chuckled as I grabbed my bag and pulled the door closed behind me.

~*~*~*~*~

"Th-thanks," I said, teeth chattering in the chill of the February, Seattle morning as I got off Victor's Harley. He'd bought it used, but it was nice, it was fast and it got him where he needed to go quick. As I tried getting my shivering under control, at that moment I wished he'd opted for a car because scrubs definitely did not protect against the cold.

He grinned. "Any time, baby sister."

"Sorry I c-cut your morning short," I said, shivering as I took off my helmet and handed it to him with a shaking hand.

"Don't be. She wasn't worth it anyway." He took the helmet clipping it onto the bar behind the seat.

I looked at him wondering if he'd ever settle down, afraid he was following in our father's footsteps. Vic was four years older than I, and at twenty-five, he was the same age Dad had been when he'd promptly cut out on us, leaving to be with one of the many women with which he'd had an affair. Oh, but thank God Dad—who was a career Army man—had stuck around long enough to give us what he called our *military names*, for which I was eternally grateful. Yeaaahh. I mean, who in their right mind with the last name of Justice, named their kids Victor and Honor? Lord. Anyway, since I'd come to live with Vic three years prior, there'd been an endless string of women in and out of his bedroom, never the same one twice, and this worried me.

There *had* been a time before the revolving door to his bedroom began, though, when he'd hooked up for almost a year with my best friend Krystal when she and I were freshman at the University of Washington. I wasn't sure what'd happened between them that'd led to their breakup as neither felt the need to clue me in—Krystal telling me she didn't feel comfortable talking with me about my brother and it wasn't like Vic would share anyway—but something had gone wrong and they hadn't spoken to each other since.

"S-so, you think you could take Betsy in somewhere?" I now asked rubbing my hands up and down my arms as I danced from foot to foot trying to ward off the cold.

"I'll see what I can do. Probably take it to Powers 'cause I know them."

"Thanks. I'll pay for it. That's not a problem. And I'll hitch a ride to the nursing home after class too so you don't have to pick me up."

He gazed at me for a moment. "Who you gonna get a ride from?"

"I'll, um, call Krys. She'll take me."

I watched his hazel eyes—the same color as mine—narrow, a flash of hurt sparking in them for a split second before they went hard. "Yeah. You do that."

"'Kay," I answered, biting my tongue to keep from asking him—for the umpteenth time—exactly what'd gone wrong between them. "Thanks."

"Yep," he replied.

I leaned in and kissed his cheek telling him goodbye then made my way quickly to class, the roar of his bike buzzing in my ears as he drove away.

~*~*~*~*~

I sat in my pathophysiology class, one of my undergraduate courses that would hopefully lead to my being an occupational therapist someday, soaking up the information my professor was raining down on me, and as usual felt tremendously lucky that I was there. The only reason I could afford college was that Dad had transferred his GI Bill towards my education—one of the few decent gestures he'd made toward Vic and me. So that and the various grants and scholarships I'd received, along with my working since I'd been in eighth grade and saving as much as I could, had helped pay for school. Vic could've used the money from Dad too, but he hadn't been interested in furthering his education, barely making it out of high school where he'd been bored to death except for playing sports, but I always knew I wanted something more.

At a pause in the lecture, I texted Krystal.

Text Message—Mon, Feb 15, 8:09 a.m.

Me: Could you give me a ride to Colonial Manor after class?

Krys: Yep. You get out at 11?

Me: Yes. THANK YOU! I'll bake you turtle brownies ;)

Krys: Yes, yes, you will lol

Me: You know it!

Krys: See you in a bit

Me: You're the best <3

Krystal and I had been best friends since fifth grade. She'd been through the David-who-punched-Mom-every-time-he-was-angry-whether-it-was-her-fault-or-not-two-years, the Brad-who-cheated-the-entire-four-months-four-months, the Wayne-who-was-an-alcoholic-but-hid-it-well-year-and-twelve-days, and finally the Albert-seven-months-and-I-had-no-idea-how-much-longer-he'd-been-in-the-picture-because-I'd-gotten-the-hell-out-of-there times with me. All of these men had been Vic and my stepdads.

The last one, Albert, was an ambulance chaser who made a ton of money taking every personal injury case he thought he could win, but he didn't shy away from civil suits either. He even had commercials—touting himself as Seattle's best attorney, which was a joke—that ran on TV late at night. He'd given me the creeps from the first time I'd met him, and when I'd voiced my misgivings to Mom, she'd replied that I was just jealous. Um, okay. You know, because I *so* wanted a forty-five-year-old controlling jerk who flirted with other women and *me*—shudder—right in front of my mother.

The summer after I'd graduated high school, one night when Mom had been working a double shift as a nurse, Albert had come into the bathroom, without my knowledge, while I'd showered. I'd just turned off the water and pulled open the curtain to see him standing there holding a towel out to me, which had made me yelp and cover myself with my hands before grabbing the towel from him, wanting to throw up at the lurid leer he'd given me.

Gross. Gross. *Gross!*

I'd screamed at him to get out, and hearing him chuckle darkly as he left, the salacious sneer on his face as he pulled the door closed, had made my fucking skin crawl. I'd quickly gone to my room and in tears had called Victor who'd been furious and told me to "pack my shit" that he'd be there as soon as he could get someone to cover him behind the bar. He'd shown up thirty minutes later ready to "stomp a mudhole" in Albert's ass, which he hadn't even ended up getting one good punch in because Albert had been smart, knowing I'd call my brother, and called the police before Vic had even shown up. Victor almost got arrested, but after telling the cops my side of the story, they'd questioned Albert who, of course, had denied the entire incident.

Victor and I had left but only after Vic told Albert he'd kick his ass if he ever saw him again.

Then my brother had gone and made things worse by posting fliers in the bar's bathrooms with Albert's picture on them and "Pedophile" printed underneath. Vic had almost gotten fired when Albert had called the bar manager to complain, threatening to sue for libel. Vic had explained to Jerry Finch, his boss, what'd happened between Albert and me, and since Mr. Finch had daughters of his own, it pissed him off what Albert had done to me; also, Vic had worked there for two years always picking up shifts when people called in, so Finch let it go, thank God.

The worst thing about it all was that Albert vowed he'd get Vic back no matter what, but Vic assured me he was only bluffing.

Later, when I'd called Mom to tell her about what'd happened, she'd blamed me for not locking the bathroom door, which I'd sworn to her that I had. She hadn't believed me, and we hadn't spoken since.

Krystal had stood beside me throughout everything, wanting to kill Albert for what he'd done—I think their protective instincts over me were what had brought her and Victor together—but I'd have done the same for her. Not that she'd be subjected to anything that disgusting since her parents were happily married, thank God.

Anyway, I loved her like a sister and would do anything for her, being my entire point.

When class was over, I waited outside the building until Krystal pulled up in her BMW. Yeah, her parents were wealthy, but you'd never know it by the way she and her family behaved. They were the most down-to-earth people I'd ever met and treated me as if I were their own.

"I owe you," I said as I got in, putting my bag on the floor in front of me.

"I'm only taking biochem at night, so our schedules work out perfectly. You owe me nothing," she replied with a chuckle as she put the car in gear.

"Probably true," I cracked, laughing when she gave me a look as we drove off. "Because you know there *was* the time I lied for you when you got an 'F' on that science paper and I told your parents everyone did bad on it even though I made a ninety-eight."

"That was in seventh grade, Honor! Jesus. Isn't there a statute of limitations on this shit?"

I chuckled. "Nope."

"Great. I get the best friend with the memory of a fucking elephant," she mumbled, as she flipped her turn signal.

"Ooohh! There's also the time you played Seven Minutes in Heaven. In the closet. With Bruce Hobwell at Amber Willis's birthday party in eighth grade." I looked at her and nodded grinning, as I let her know I *did* have a long memory.

"Bruce. Isn't he in jail now?" I laughed when she made a face.

"Don't forget sophomore year when you snuck out of your house to make out with Jace Jones, and I covered your ass telling your mom you'd come to my house because I was upset that my mom and I had a fight." I paused for a moment and frowned. "Damn. I feel bad for lying to your parents." I saw her shake her head and roll her eyes. "But I do have a lot of shit on you."

She cut her eyes at me before turning them back to the street as she exited campus. "Don't think I don't have plenty of shit on you too, girly."

I shrugged with a chuckle. "Who you gonna tell? Victor?" I realized my mistake immediately when I saw her face fall. I tried so hard never to mention him to her, but it was tough sometimes not to do so because first, he was my brother and second, I lived with him. "Damn it.

I'm sorry, Krys." When she ignored me, my frustrations came out. "I wish you'd just tell me what the hell went on with you two so I could stop pussyfooting around this shit all the time!"

She let out a huff as she drove then flipped her blond hair behind her shoulder, a clear sign she was annoyed.

"If you'd just tell me..." I repeated, hating that she was keeping secrets from me.

"I don't wanna talk about it right now." She shrugged. "Besides, he's banging everyone and their dog nowadays, so it really doesn't matter."

"You know, I'd tell you if it were me," I declared, a little pissed off that she was still holding on to it.

"I'll tell you one day. It just still kinda...hurts."

We were right back to the conversation we'd had so many times, so I dropped it. It only upset her and angered me, so yeah.

"So, I had a date last night," she shared, thankfully changing the topic.

And this had become another routine of ours since she and Vic broke up—Krystal telling me about her disastrous dates then we'd laugh about them.

She was gorgeous with all her long, blond hair, blue eyes, bubbly personality and trim five-foot-five self, and it was a given she was going to get asked out. I just hated that she accepted almost every offer she received. But she assured me she was having fun and loved meeting new people, and she did come back with some very interesting stories, so no harm, no foul, I supposed.

Although I knew what she was really doing was searching for Vic's replacement, just as I guessed he was trying to replace her with all the women he brought home, I was always willing to listen, hoping she might actually find someone who was good enough for her.

"Yeah?" I couldn't help but smile knowing something bad was coming.

"This guy looked like Tom Austen from *The Royals*!" she said.

"Really? Jasper's so hot!" I squealed, excited that maybe it'd been a good date for a change.

"Well, if Jasper had a bald spot and found out he'd reached his credit card limit when he went to pay for dinner." She burst out laughing.

I giggled with her. "Oh, no. Not again."

"I'm gonna go broke paying for all these dates," she said with a snort.

As we pulled up to Colonial Manor, the nursing home where I'd worked for two years, I put my hand on the door handle and turned to her. "I'm always here for you. I'd never judge you, you know that, right?"

She tilted her head toward me as if to say *Duh* and answered, "I know you wouldn't."

"And I hope you find what you're looking for," I added.

At her melancholy look and knowing our conversation was over, I opened the door, grabbing my bag as I did. "Thanks again for the ride. One of these days, I'll be rich and have a Mercedes and will be able to give you rides too."

She chuckled. "I know you will. And I can't wait."

CHAPTER 2

"You could be such a beautiful girl, Holly. I just don't understand why you don't make yourself more presentable," Mrs. Johnson—who I was sure came from money, her genteel affect clear as day as she looked at me disapprovingly—bemoaned as she patted my hand.

Then upon remembering she was too proper to show compassion, she removed her hand from mine using it to smooth her hair back toward the tight, white bun that sat neatly at the base of her neck. As she slicked her hair back, her head came up regally and sitting up straighter she looked me up and down, taking in my scrubs.

I got ready to sustain another round of criticism. Yay.

The good thing was, she was fourth from the last of my rounds of the day, so while I walked the wings, I had plenty of time to prepare for her less-than-flattering appraisals.

Finding her meds on the cart, I held back my snort knowing she would only chastise me if I let out such an unladylike sound. But the fact was, we had a similar conversation every day, her dementia making her think she was talking to her niece. Sad thing about it all was, everything she said to "Holly" usually hit home with me; therefore, I had to take her comments lightly because even though I felt I had a good balance of self-esteem, I might've become somewhat insecure since I was exposed to them on an almost-daily basis.

"There's so much you could do." She looked sympathetically at my auburn hair that was up in the usual ponytail. "Maybe if you did something with your hair, it would make you appear...prettier."

I self-consciously grabbed my ponytail and ran my hand down it holding the cup out toward her.

"And a little bit of makeup wouldn't hurt," she said as an afterthought. Jeez.

Even though I knew she wasn't speaking to me in particular, she was right. But, hell, I was working! Ugh.

I sighed, playing the part, looking down at the small paper cup I held in my hand that had her daily pills in it. "I know, Aunt Greta. You're right."

She smiled. "See? That's a good start, Holly."

I returned her smile as she took the small paper container which she tipped up to let the pills fall into her mouth. I next helped her hold her water cup so she could drink.

"Now, you go tell Robert he was a fool to ever let you go," she advised with a definitive nod.

"I will," I replied.

"That's a good girl." She handed me the pill dispenser.

I wadded it up and threw it away telling her goodbye and pushing the med cart out of her room, moved to Mr. Avery's room next door.

"Hello, Oswald," I said as I knocked before going inside. I knew he loved it when I called him by his first name because he'd asked me to do so a jillion times until I'd finally consented.

"Hi, Honor! My goodness, you're looking lovely today!"

Ah. Much better.

"You're not looking so bad yourself," I replied with a grin. I loved that he was so sprightly and alert. And nice. We'd had many conversations ranging from whether the moon landing was real to when Lady Gaga's next album would drop, regular visits from his teenage granddaughters helping to keep him in the loop of current events and the rest because he was sharp as a tack.

"I did twenty pushups today," he bragged. "Tomorrow I'm going for twenty-five!"

"Wow! Good for you! I doubt I could do even five," I said with a snort as I held his cup out to him. I swore he was ninety-five going on thirty. "It's time to take your vitamins."

He took the cup pouring the pills into his mouth then taking the water, washed them down. "Ahhh!" he breathed out. "Good as new now."

"That's right," I declared.

"The girls are coming tomorrow to challenge me in a two-on-one pickup basketball game," he informed.

"Oh, I'm sure you can take them."

"I averaged thirty-two points a game in college," he said proudly.

"That's awesome! I'll bet you still have it too."

He nodded. "Taught Annabeth everything she knows, especially about shooting. Now she's averaging twenty-one. The last game they took me to, I got to see her score thirty-eight."

"Dang!" I exclaimed. "Takes after her grandpa, doesn't she?"

"That she does," he answered with a smile.

"You figure out the first move yet?" I asked, nodding to his ever-present chessboard. He was constantly trying out new opening moves. When I had free time, which wasn't very often, I tried coming in and playing a quick game with him.

"Not yet. You found your knight yet?" he asked with a grin. It'd become sort of a running joke between us when he'd once referred to the queen as "Pearl." At my questioning look, he'd explained he meant his wife who'd passed away five years before. "Pearl was my queen," he'd uttered, getting a wistful look. Then he'd told me I needed to hold out for my knight and one day he'd become my king.

I now smiled. "Not yet. I'm still waiting for him."

"He'll show, beautiful girl."

I smiled. "Have a great day, Oswald. I'll see you tomorrow!"

"Yes, you will," he announced with a wink as he sat in his chair, settling in to study the board.

I continued on my rounds having only two more rooms to stop in, so glad that I had my CNA and had just gotten my certification to hand out medications the previous month. I now got to deliver meds to the patients who could administer them themselves, and I enjoyed seeing them every day. It also kept me from doing what I'd done previously which had involved feeding patients and changing diapers. I mean, I was okay with doing those things, it's just that the latter hadn't been too much fun and this was so much easier.

~*~*~*~*~

Thirty minutes before I got off work, Victor texted to let me know he'd pick me up. After finishing charts, I waited at the door then saw him ride up on his bike.

"Hey," I said as I put on my helmet. "You take Betsy in?"

"Yep," he answered.

My hands paused at the straps and I gave him a grouchy look. "And?"

He chuckled. "Tomorrow."

"They say what's wrong with her?"

"Carburetor."

I rolled my eyes at his not-so-glib answers. "Good." After getting on the bike, I asked, "They think they can fix her?"

"Yep," he supplied as we took off.

My brother. A veritable fount of info.

~*~*~*~*~

"Hello?" I called inside the empty service area at Powers Automotive.

It was a quarter to six the next evening, and Vic had dropped me off telling me he had to get to work. So now there I stood in a deserted auto shop wondering if I was going to have to call a cab to get home. I'd seen my truck sitting outside the place but the keys hadn't been in it.

As I looked around, I saw their hours posted on the wall showing they were open until six but no one was around. Great. Walking to a door and looking through the small window in it, I viewed the garage where a couple cars were up on hydraulics but no one was inside there either. Then thinking someone might be inside, I pushed opened the door and yelled out another hello but still got no answer.

"Damn it," I mumbled as I let the door fall shut. Realizing I'd have to come back tomorrow and upon turning to go, I ran smack-dab into a hard wall of chest covered by a grease-stained denim shirt. "Shit!" I bit out with a jump. "You scared me!" My eyes traced up over broad shoulders, a strong Adam's apple—can Adam's apples even *be* strong?—,a chiseled stubble-covered jawline, before landing on the face of a freaking Greek god and my mouth dropped open.

Holy. Wow.

As I stood staring up at Mr. Hot Mechanic Dude, I watched in fascination as his golden eyes twinkled in amusement.

"I'm, uh, and I'm here to, uh," I stammered trying to remember who I was and why I was there, the presence of this hottie suddenly making me inarticulate. Ergh.

One side of his mouth now drew up into a smirk and I saw his body shift a bit, as if he was used to this sort of reaction from women. Like he knew his good looks had me tongue-tied.

Well, check that. Mr. Hot *Jerk* Mechanic Dude.

While I stood there trying to get a handle on what I wanted to say, he wasn't helping out one bit. Nope. All he did next was grin, and I knew he was waiting to see if a complete sentence might actually be able to form its way out of my stupid mouth.

Then he scanned my body with those honey-colored eyes of his winking at me after he finished his perusal.

Double check that. Mr. Hot *Bastard* Mechanic Dude.

Oh. Goody.

I took a deep breath then looking to his side, focused on a calendar on the wall, one that had a girl in a barely-there bikini splayed across the hood of a car, my thoughts being that if his gorgeousness wasn't all up in my face, I might be able to speak correctly. "My brother dropped off my truck yesterday. It's sitting outside so I think it's ready?"

"Eyes here, sweetheart," I heard him command quietly.

Blinking away from the calendar thinking I must've misunderstood him, I looked up to see the smuggest look ever settled right there on his handsome face.

"Excuse me?" I questioned testily.

"Were you speakin' to me?" he asked, eyebrows raised, his look getting even more superior, if that could be believed.

I frowned and couldn't help snapping, "Since you're the only other person here, I guess I am."

He laughed low. "Figured that one out all on your own, did ya?"

Huh. He really was a jerk. And I pegged him for exactly who he was. He was one of those pretty boys who knew it. I'd seen my own brother act this way—evasive, cocky—with women and had laughed at them for falling for it. Well, I wasn't like them. I had this under control, piece of cake. Easy peasy.

Or so I thought.

Indifference washed over me and a bored look covered my face as I said, "Is my truck ready or not?"

"Is it in the garage?" he questioned, eyebrow raised. When I shook my head, he asked, "It sitting outside?"

"Yep," I drawled, popping the *P* at the end of the word.

"Then I'd say, *yep*, it's ready." He mocked me by popping the *P* too, and the arrogant look he gave me had me gritting my teeth.

More than ready to go home—and wanting to get away from this pompous ass—I asked with a sigh, "How much do I owe?"

"No charge," he concluded, holding out his palm which held my keys.

My eyes narrowed suspiciously as I echoed, "No charge?"

He grinned. "You heard correctly."

I huffed out a breath. "May I ask why?"

"You sure can."

Crickets.

God.

I now full-on glared at him tired of his ridiculous way of communicating. "Why?"

He chuckled. "It's an old carburetor. We've got plenty of them around the shop."

He still hadn't explained why I didn't have to at least pay for labor.

"And?" I prompted, more than aggravated now.

He shrugged. "And…no charge."

I crossed my arms on my chest. "I can't *not* pay you."

He crossed his arms too. "Only took about thirty minutes."

Ooookay. Because that explained it all.

I employed his silent act, looking at him until he was finally forced to continue. "Carburetors are simple. No charge."

My brow wrinkled for a moment as I thought it over. Not paying didn't sit well with me because if I'd learned anything from watching my mother, I knew that you never got something for nothing since each of my stepdads seemed to have come with a fricking price. So making a decision, I reached into my purse, grabbed my wallet and pulling out my debit card held it out toward him, shaking my head. "I can't."

I saw the annoyance in his eyes that threatened to overthrow his smartass demeanor for just a moment until the cockiness returned. "You can hold that thing out there all night long, sweetheart; not gonna do you any good."

Dang it! I bit the inside of my lip wondering if this was too good to be true as I reluctantly put my wallet away. I crossed my arms again still not good with not having to pay, but if I didn't have to, that meant I'd have some extra spending cash for the week which made me want to smile.

Until he spoke again.

"Plus, you've got a great rack." He canted his head to the side, mockingly biting his lip, as his eyes dropped to my chest before coming back up to meet mine. "So, yeah, no charge."

My arms fell to my sides at the same time my mouth unlatched and just hung open. When the shock subsided a bit, I whispered, "Did you really just say that?"

"Yep." More popping—jerk!—then he gave me a smirk and grabbing one of my hands pulled it up and placed the keys in it. "I'm assuming you're smart enough to find your way out?" he said, jerking his head toward the front door. He turned and went out into the garage leaving me alone in the service area.

I stood there staring at the garage door as it closed, mouth still agape. Then shaking myself out of the stupor I was in, I mumbled, "Asshole," before leaving.

CHAPTER 3

"That guy at Powers is a jerk!" I spit into my phone which was on speaker as I drove home.

Victor laughed. "Which one was it?"

"I don't know his name! You mean there are more?"

"You probably got Drake. I played football against him with his cousin Gable Powers in high school, so I know who Drake is. And, yeah, he's got brothers."

"His last name is Powers? As in they actually own the garage?" I'd been thinking the name Powers just meant the mechanics were powerful or something. Boy, I was a sharp one.

"Mm hm."

"And are these brothers all insensitive assholes like him?"

"Probably." I heard Vic snort.

Wonderful. There were more Powers brothers. And they were like him. Yippee.

"He said I had a great rack!" I whisper-hissed into the phone which made my brother crack up laughing. "It's not funny, Vic! It's called sexual harassment!"

Through his following chuckles, he said, "Hey, not saying it's right but he could've said something rude."

"That *was* rude! God!"

"Lighten up, On. He's not a bad guy."

"Seemed that way to me," I grumbled.

About that time, Betsy rattled making a *ca-chunk!* noise, dying just as I was in the middle of making a right turn.

"Shit!" I yelled.

"What?"

"Betsy died!" I coasted on around the corner into a parking lot then tried starting my truck but to no avail. "No! Come on!" I cried, turning the ignition again a few more times.

"Is it making a clicking noise? Might be the battery," Vic offered.

"No. Listen." I set my phone on the dash so he could hear the *wurrrhh wurrrhh wurrrhh* sound it was making. "Hear it?"

"Could be the distributor cap. Where are you? I'll call the garage again. They can tow it back."

Great. I could only hope, what was his name again, oh, yeah, Drake, would be the one to show.

I told Vic my location then waited to see Mr. Charm again.

~*~*~*~*~

"So, you have brothers? At least that's what my brother told me," I asked the guy I now knew was Drake Powers while he looked around under the hood of my truck with a flashlight. I also might've admired how his broad shoulders V'd down into narrow hips for a moment but we won't discuss that.

It had only taken him about ten minutes to get to where I was stranded which was good. I wasn't too familiar with the area but it was dark and a few questionable characters had walked by while I'd waited inside my truck, a few of them giving me leers which had made me uncomfortable. I'd let out a breath of relief when Drake had pulled up behind me in a white tow truck that had *Powers Automotive* painted in red on the sides.

He'd gotten out, walked to my window, stood there looking at me, eyebrows raised, until I'd rolled down the window.

"Pop the hood and stay inside," he'd instructed, then moved to the front of my truck to unlatch the hood.

I'd frowned, mumbling, "Jerk," as I pulled on the lever. But after a couple minutes of sitting in the cab, I'd gotten bored, so at the risk of being yelled at, I joined him. And now I was trying to get him to talk, maybe fix our getting off to a bad start. I mean, although he'd been rude, he had repaired my truck for free and was now working on it again. The least I could do was be nice and let him know I appreciated it.

"I've got four brothers," he answered my question distractedly, as I watched his hands jiggling something on the engine in the light from the flashlight that was sitting off to the side.

Huh. No smartass comment from him. Well, look at us conversing!

That is until he went on. "And you have a brother," he kept messing with something under the hood. "Got a lot in common. We should get married."

What an ass.

He now stood and gazed down at me pulling a rag from his back pocket wiping his hands with it. "You ever listen?"

My eyes narrowed. What the heck did that mean?

He nodded slowly as if he had me all figured out. "Told you no charge and you argued. Said to stay in the truck. Look where you are." He took a second to scrutinize me again before asking, "So do you?"

God. This guy was just...rude! I scowled as I snipped, "I'm twenty-two, not five! You can't tell me what to do!"

And now I sounded like I was five. Shit.

He snorted. "Uh huh."

I was sick of this, tired of feeling bad about myself around him. "I'm a nice person!" I suddenly blurted, arms stretched pathetically out in front of me, palms up as if pleading with him to believe me.

"I'm sure you are," he muttered apathetically, moving past me and walking back to the tow truck.

And look at me, following him. *And* continuing to talk. Ugh. "I am! We just got off on the wrong foot! If you got to know me, you'd like me!"

"That so?" he asked flippantly, opening the door to the tow truck and getting in. He next started it, put it into gear and pulled out into the traffic lane making me jump out of the way as he drove to the front of my truck and backed up to it.

Huh. It was then that I gave up trying to be friendly with him because, you know, when someone tries to run you over, you're probably not going to be friends.

I huffed out a breath then stomped to meet him at the front of my truck. "You almost hit me!"

"Told you to stay in your truck for a reason."

Damn it. He was right.

Resignedly I asked, "So what's wrong with it?"

As he lowered the wheel lift at the back of the tow truck, he explained in his aloof way, "Distributor cap."

"That's what my brother thought," I remarked softly.

He remained quiet as did I while he hooked up my truck. When he finished, I was already moving to the passenger side of the tow when he ordered, "Get in," which just made me roll my eyes but whatever.

Needless to say, we didn't speak on the drive back to the garage. When we arrived, I got out watching as he opened one of the garage doors, backed Betsy in, detached her from the tow then parked the big truck at the side of the building. While he did this, I called Krystal who said she'd come get me.

Drake walked over and unlocked the service area door. "Should be ready tomorrow evening. Got a ride coming?" At my nod, he continued. "You can wait in here."

I walked in ahead of him then turned to see him push a few buttons on the alarm panel disarming it I assumed. Then he went out into the garage leaving me to wait alone.

~*~*~*~*~

The next morning, Krystal picked me up for class.

"I owe you so big. Fucking hell," I muttered before taking a drink of the coffee she'd brought for me.

"Someone's in a good mood," she said as we drove across town to campus.

"Yeah, well, if Betsy would stop breaking down, I might be in a better mood."

"What was wrong with her?"

"Some kinda cap."

She snorted. "Look at me, acting like I care about engines."

This made me chuckle. "I wondered about that when you asked."

"But I do hope this fixes it," she offered. "Not that I mind picking you up," she added. "I just know you hate having to depend on someone."

"I hope it does too. Then I can stop bugging you all the time."

"You're not bugging me, On. We've been besties for a decade. I couldn't make it without you."

"Same," I answered, taking a drink. "But you should see the mechanic, Krys. He's freaking hot," I shared. "But he's—"

"You should ask him out!" she interrupted.

"—a huge jerk," I finished.

She sighed. "Why're all the hot ones jerks?"

"Because they can be. I mean, look at Vic." I stopped myself and mumbled, "Damn it. I did it again. Sorry."

"You know what? Don't be," she said. "I thought about it last night. We've avoided this for two years now. He's your brother. You're bound to talk about him. And I need to suck it up."

"You sure? It is kinda hard not mentioning him every now and then."

"Yep. I'm sure. Don't worry about it, honey."

When we got to the campus, I told her I'd call Vic to come get me, but she said she had to talk to a couple professors and would be around, so she'd take me to work. I tried giving her gas money but she'd given me a look, so I'd put my wallet away.

"I'll pay you back someday," I said getting out of her car.

"You will when we're old ladies living together and you have to wipe my butt," she claimed with a giggle, getting out of the car and closing her door.

"Gross. Thanks for the nice sendoff."

"Anytime!"

~*~*~*~*~

"So, kinesiology was fun today," I told Krystal as she drove me to Colonial Manor after class.

"Oh, yeah?"

"Professor Banks took us to the gymnastics training center where he proceeded to hang from the horizontal bar. You ready for this?"

"What'd he do?"

I shuddered remembering it. "He dislocated both of his friggin' shoulders!"

"What? Ew!"

"I know! *Pop! Pop!* and then he just hung there!" I shivered again. Ick!

"And his point?"

"We're talking about ball and socket joints right now. Apparently, he's dislocated both of his shoulders in accidents before, so now he can just slip those suckers out."

"That's disgusting," she commented.

"Tell me. You didn't have to watch it. Or not be able to look away when he had his teaching assistant put them back in."

"How in the world did he do that?"

"He helped Banks lie on the floor on his stomach then the guy stood over him and pulled each shoulder back until they went back in. Ugh. Worst demo ever."

"That's pretty bad."

"Felt like I was watching some bad medieval torture film," I commented.

"Or *Game of Thrones* in 3D, all up-close and personal."

We looked at each other and at the same time cried, "Theon!" as we pulled up to the nursing home.

"Now I'm all sad about Theon. Thanks for that nice sendoff," she mumbled, repeating my earlier quip.

As I got out, I turned and retorted, "Paybacks!" and laughed when she made a face as I closed the car door.

Mrs. Johnson had been in a mood and wouldn't talk to me, only muttering something about Robert not being worthy and that lipstick would help. Pretty sure she meant me, er, Holly. Whatever.

I'd left her room and gone into Mr. Avery's where he was busy playing a game of chess with himself.

"Now that looks like a win-win," I said with a chuckle.

He looked up and smiled. "No, you see, that side is Hector, my son-in-law. He beats me every time I go visit. I'm trying to figure out how to counter his moves." He held his phone up to me which had a website displayed. "Found out he's using the Ruy Lopez opening." He looked down at the board. "Now all I've got to do is find what works. The Berlin Defense is what I usually do, but I blow it." He scratched his head. "Maybe if I tried the Schliemann or Classical..."

I studied the board for a moment. "Maybe BxC6?"

He stared at the pieces. "You know, that just might work." He moved the pawn to take the knight and smiled. "Ol' Hector's in for a surprise next time I play him. Thanks, smart girl."

I chuckled. "Any time, Oswald. Here're your vitamins."

We both knew they weren't vitamins, but he'd confided once that he hated taking pills. So to make him feel better, I'd just started calling them that and the problem had gone away.

"Ahh, brain power," he said after swallowing them down. Then looking up at me he asked, "You found him yet?"

I chuckled. "Not yet."

"He's out there." He looked back at the board, making the move I suggested. "And he'll sweep you off your feet soon." He looked up and winked.

"I'll keep waiting then," I replied with a smile. "See you later! Good luck figuring the rest out!" I called as I left his room, seeing that he was already back to analyzing the board.

When I finished my rounds, I checked my phone seeing that Vic had texted saying he'd pick me up then drop me off at Powers. I was grabbing my coat from the back room when Alex, another CNA, came up to the desk.

"If I have to change one more diaper..." he mumbled. Alex was short and muscular, his flawless skin the color of coffee. He wore his hair in a faux-hawk with a fade and had a trim beard, both always groomed impeccably. I snorted and he gave me a look. "Don't even start in on telling me to get my meds certification. I'm hoping I'll get accepted this time and can say *adios* to this place."

He and I had started working at Colonial Manor at the same time and he'd been rejected twice now for nursing school; however, he'd reapplied a couple weeks ago.

"You'll do it!" I assured. "You're too good not to go. I'm sending you good vibes you'll get in this time." I fluttered my fingers at him as I backed down the hallway for the door where I'd heard Vic's motorcycle roaring up.

"That better work, or I'm holding you personally responsible!" he hollered after me making me laugh.

"Hey!" I said to my brother, grabbing the helmet he held out to me and putting it on.

"Hey yourself," he replied.

"Hopefully, this is the last time you have to take me to Powers," I muttered as I climbed on the back of his bike. "But I'm making chicken tetrazzini, your favorite, tonight so you'll have something to eat when you get home."

"Sounds good. But not at four in the morning. I'll eat it tomorrow before I go in," he replied.

"I'll save you a plate!" I answered above the rumbling as we took off.

CHAPTER 4

An older version of Drake was behind the desk in the service area at Powers Automotive when I went inside after Vic dropped me off, and I figured he had to be Drake's dad. Dang. These Powers men were handsome!

"Can I help you?" he asked.

"Yes, my truck's outside, so I think it's ready?"

He glanced down to the desktop then picked up a piece of paper reading the top of it. "Justice?" he asked.

"Yes."

He went back to reading then glanced up at me. "No charge for the distributor cap today, but I went ahead and ordered a new idler pulley and serpentine belt. You wanna get those fixed. We're also gonna check out your fuel pump just to make sure it's working right."

I nodded. Yay. More repairs.

"Parts should be in next week, probably by Wednesday, so if you wanna bring her back in that morning that'd be good. It'll take a couple days so you can pick 'er up on Friday evening. We'll give you a call to let you know if the parts get here sooner."

"Oh, okay. Thank you. Do you have any idea how much it'll cost?"

He clicked some keys on the computer. "Looking at around three hundred."

I had a little over three thousand in my savings account that I added to monthly, so it wasn't that I didn't have enough money. I just hated dipping into it since I was saving to get a new car! Oh, the irony. Also, having to come back and possibly seeing Drake again was less than appealing, but since Betsy needed to be fixed, I would.

"All right. And that should be all the work she needs for now?" I asked.

"Brake pads are looking worn and we need to check the rotors," he replied with a raised eyebrow.

"Are those important?" I questioned dumbly.

"Yes, I'd say they're pretty important, hon. If you bring it in tomorrow morning, you can pick it up Friday night."

"Um, how much will that cost?"

"If it's just the pads and on both axles, we're looking at around a hundred bucks. If it's just the front axle, it's half that."

"Okay." I could handle that and if it kept me from having to come back here again, it'd be well worth it. Well, after that other stuff was done next week. Jeez. "And you're sure there's no charge for today?" I inquired.

Just then the garage door opened and I heard a woman giggling. Turning, I saw a smiling Drake—smiling!—come walking in behind a cute little brunette...as he checked out her ass in her tight jeans.

"Dad, Dina's out of blinker fluid again," Drake said with a snort.

"Matt, if you'd just sell me a bottle and show me how to put it in, I wouldn't have to keep coming by to see you hot Powers men all the time! This is the third time this month," the Dina chick said with another giggle to the man behind the counter who I'd now learned was Matt, and had guessed right that he was Drake's dad. Dina appeared to be in her late thirties and she was very cute. And apparently, a mechanic groupie.

I saw Matt's eyebrows come up as he looked at his son. "Blinker fluid?" he questioned.

Drake laughed which made me smile to see he had a playful side to him other than the assholish one he'd displayed toward me. But my smile disappeared quickly when his eyes suddenly landed on mine and I watched as his face went hard.

What was his problem with me? God.

I turned back to Matt. "So no charge for today?" I repeated.

His eyes dropped to the paper on the desk. "That's right. Bring it in in the morning and we'll get you fixed up." He pulled my keys from a hook on the wall behind him and handed them to me.

"Thanks." I turned to leave but Drake blocked my way. "Excuse me," I said, trying to maneuver around him.

"You're coming in tomorrow morning?" he asked making me look up at him.

"Yes," I answered flatly making another move to leave.

"Why don't you just leave it. Get a ride home. It'd be the *smart* thing to do," he pointed out in a surly tone.

I wanted to say, "Ya think?" then explain that I was tired of having other people give me rides. But I held it in and only muttered, "Yep," making sure to pop that fucking P, just before I walked out.

~*~*~*~*~

At home while I made the chicken tetrazzini, my phone rang.

"Please tell me this was a good one," I answered, putting my phone on speaker as I drained the noodles.

Krystal laughed. "You're gonna love this. So I meet him at Saki, right? We're chatting over our sushi, having a good ol' time, when suddenly he jumps up and yells, 'My parole officer's here!' and sprints out of the place."

"He did not!" I gasped.

"Yep. Best part about it? I looked around at the other patrons nearby, shrugged and continued eating." She let out a whoop as she cracked up.

I laughed too. "Good lord, Krys. Are there any good ones out there?"

Through her giggles, she declared, "I'm thinking not at this point."

"Come over and eat chicken tetrazzini with me."

"I just ate!"

"Sushi! You'll be hungry in an hour," I claimed with a chuckle.

"True. Uh, is Vic—"

"He's working. Come on over. I'm making my sour-cream chocolate cake too," I tempted.

"Be there in ten!" she said and rang off.

~*~*~*~*~

"And just before he bounced, he told me he was a spy for the CIA."

Krystal had continued regaling me with details from her latest failed date once she got to the house.

"God. Where do you find these guys?" I asked.

"This guy was actually pretty hot, believe it or not. I met him at Best Buy, which he explained tonight, just before he went on the lam," she snorted, "that the reason he'd been there was he was emailing the CIA so Russia couldn't trace the ISP back to his laptop." She cracked up.

"You've got to be kidding me." I shook my head snickering as I cleared our dishes off the table.

"Nope. Oh! I'm gonna look him up," she said, picking up her phone. As I cut the cake and put it on plates, she shrieked, "Wow! He really is a criminal! He robbed a store! Look! It says, 'Charges Pending,' for Office Depot." She held her phone out to me and I shook my head as I set her plate in front of her.

"So when you met him in Best Buy, he was probably casing the joint then," I declared with a giggle.

She threw her head back and laughed. "Probably! I should see if they'll give me a gift card or something for thwarting a crime!"

"It's the least they can do," I stated sardonically.

We ate our cake on the couch, watching an episode of *The Girlfriend Experience* that I'd DVR'd, with Krystal commenting the entire time, "Oh, God, he's so gross. How can she be with him? I could never do that," to which I wholeheartedly agreed.

Before leaving, she told me she'd meet me at the auto shop in the morning, but not until after I wrapped up two pieces of cake for her to take home.

~*~*~*~*~

I dropped Betsy off the next morning, giving Matt the keys at the desk. I then went outside to wait for Krystal because apparently, a man inside had eaten sardines or something fishy for breakfast and the smell was grossing me out.

As I waited, I heard an agitated voice coming from the side of the shop saying, "You signed...yeah, I know...you were gone...I'm trying...that's horse shit! I said I'm trying..."

Drake. Great.

Before I could make a move, he walked out where I could see him, his back to me as he kept talking.

"Uh huh. Yeah, I know."

I wavered between going inside with Mr. Fishy or acting like I was talking on my own phone and not listening to him when he turned to see me standing there, frozen in my indecision.

Shit!

"Gotta go," he said. Lifting the tail of his denim shirt and jamming his phone into his back jeans pocket, he walked toward me with the usual pissed-off look on his face. "Get an earful?"

"I wasn't listening," I replied cooly.

His golden eyes were darker than usual as he shoved a hand through his hair. "Fucking women," he murmured then went inside the shop.

I let out an annoyed huff as Krystal pulled up.

When I got into her car she asked, "Was that the hot mechanic?" staring at Drake where he now stood inside the service area talking to his dad.

"Yeah. That's the asshole," I clued her in. "You should go out with him so you don't ruin your streak." I let out a snort.

She giggled as we pulled out of the parking lot. "Nah. I only date nice guys who are losers. Can't go changing it up now!"

~*~*~*~*~

"Maybe I should look at getting another vehicle," I complained to Alex that night at work as I pulled on my jacket. "I'm tired of my poor brother and Krystal having to haul me around everywhere."

"But the auto shop said that'll be it, right? After the pulley thing, you won't need more repairs?" he asked.

"For now." I sighed. "I was hoping she wouldn't kick the bucket until I got my master's then a good job and could afford a new car."

"Uh, that's in, like, another two years," he pointed out unnecessarily.

"Yeah. But I take good care of her, so I was hoping she'd make it."

"She might. Never know."

Changing the subject from my automotive woes, I asked him about nursing school. "When do you hear if you got in?"

"Two months. I think they make you wait on purpose just to make you sweat. It's fucking torture."

I was sure it was and I hated it for him. I patted his arm. "You'll get in this time. I know it."

He shook his head. "I don't get in this time, I'm heading to med school. Heard it's easier anyway."

I chuckled. "Could be." I heard Victor's motorcycle roaring up just then. "I'm off the next two days so I'll see you Sunday?"

"Sure thing. Take care," he hollered after me.

"You too!" I called, waving as I left.

~*~*~*~*~

Since I was tired of being a pest and bumming rides, Thursday night after getting home I texted my professor to let him know I wouldn't be in class the next morning. He texted back telling me to email him my completed assignment but to make sure to check the website for lecture notes.

Friday morning I slept in, not getting up until eight, and deciding to take it easy—after eating an overflowing bowl of Lucky Charms—lazed around on the couch catching up on my TV shows. By ten I was bored to tears, having cringed at almost every winning outfit on *Project Runway* because I'd picked the losers each time to win, and glad I hadn't majored in fashion design because that would've ended up in a big, fat fail.

Getting up off the sofa, I engaged myself by changing around the living room furniture. Which took a whopping twenty minutes. Afterward, as I was in the kitchen making a meat lasagna, another of Vic's favorites, I'd just decided that later I'd move the furniture in our bedrooms, when he walked in.

"You trying to kill me?" he asked, scratching his shirtless stomach.

"Damn. You just caught me before I put the arsenic in," I joked as I layered the ingredients in a casserole dish. I glanced at him then went back to my task. "Why do you say that?"

He got the milk out to make his own bowl of cereal. "Rearranging the furniture."

I chuckled. "Gotta keep it interesting."

"It'll be interesting when I come in one night and trip over the ottoman busting out all my teeth." He took a bite from the bowl he held in his hands giving me a look from where he leaned back against the counter.

I finished with the last layer of mozzarella and put the dish into the oven then turned to him. "Teeth are overrated."

He snorted. "Uh huh. Why're you home?"

"I'm tired of asking for rides. And with that being said, can you drop me off at Powers when you go to work tonight?"

"Yep," he garbled through a big mouthful of sugary goodness.

"Thanks." I puffed out a breath. "I owe you too. I'll never be able to pay you guys back for the rides."

"I'm your brother. I'm supposed to do shit for you." He shrugged.

"The only way I can pay you back is by feeding you," I mumbled.

He pooched his muscular belly out and patted it. "That you do. You're gonna make me fat."

I rolled my eyes. "Psh. Like that'd ever happen."

"Speaking of, gotta hit the gym. When'll that be ready?" He nodded at the oven.

"Forty-five minutes."

"Perfect," he said, putting his bowl into the sink and rinsing it out. "Be back in an hour."

He kissed the side of my head as he went by then went to change as I hollered after him, "Don't worry about me! I'll just be here making our bedrooms more interesting!"

CHAPTER 5

"Could you come with me so this Drake guy won't be a dick to me for a change?" I asked Victor when we pulled up to the auto shop where Betsy was parked outside.

He turned off his bike and we went inside walking to the front desk that Drake stood behind.

"Hey, man," Drake said with a grin—which made him look so handsome but too bad he was such a jerk—when he looked up and saw my brother. "Long time." He reached a hand over the counter and shook Vic's hand.

"Fuck, it has been," Vic answered. "Seven years since I played football with Gable." He chuckled. "Here to pick up my sister's truck," he said with a nod toward me.

"Thought it might've been some relation when I saw the last name," Drake said to Vic, then glancing at me, gave me his customary annoyed look—yay—and clicked at the computer keyboard. "Brake pads were worn on the front only," he said to Vic then looked back at the computer screen. "So that'll be fifty-three twenty-five," he uttered, not even looking at me and saying to Vic, "I'll never forget sophomore year, fucking Gable threw the winning touchdown."

Vic laughed. "Yeah. I recall you not being so bad yourself. I know I blitzed about twenty times that game and you got away."

Now Drake laughed. "If I remember right, I think you sacked me twice too. Fucker."

While they talked, I handed Drake my debit card disinterestedly, showing him that his not liking me had no bearing on me whatsoever. *Whatsoever!* But he wasn't paying a lick of attention to me anyway. Ugh. I signed the slip he put on the counter then took the keys he'd set down.

"Some guys and I get together on Sundays and play. It's just flag but with some of the meatheads it gets a little rough. If you wanna relive the glory days, we'll be at Roosevelt High School this Sunday at one. One of the guys who plays coaches there, so we get the practice field."

"That'd be cool," Vic said.

Drake glimpsed at the computer screen. "This your number on here?" When Vic nodded, Drake pulled out his phone. "I'll add you as a contact so I can get hold of you in case the game gets cancelled." He then gave Vic his number, and they grinned at each other. I couldn't help rolling my eyes thinking they reminded me of the guys in *Step Brothers* when they became besties. Ergh.

After their bromantic interlude, Vic thanked Drake, telling him he'd see him Sunday before walking outside with me.

"You good?" my brother asked as he threw a leg over his motorcycle and put on his helmet.

"Yeah," I replied, glancing back to see Drake still inside behind the desk. "You see the way he looked at me?" I whispered.

Vic laughed. "I think he likes you." He started up his bike. At my dirty look, he grinned. "I'm not shitting you." Just as he put the bike into gear, he said, "Get home. I'll see you tomorrow. And thanks again for the lasagna."

I watched as he drove away, shaking my head wondering if I'd ever understand guys. They were so weird. How in the world he could take Drake's dirty looks as his somehow liking me, I had no fricking clue. Turning back to my truck, I unlocked her, got in and started her up. As I backed out, I saw Drake glance at me offhandedly before turning back to his computer and I had to control my middle finger on the wheel from saluting him.

"That's right, asshole. Nothing here to see," I said as I put it in "Drive."

Sunday I was frying chicken for lunch when Vic came into the kitchen wearing God knew what and striking the Heisman pose.

"What do you think?" he asked.

I looked at him then back at the pan as I used tongs to move the chicken around and stated drily, "Halloween isn't for another eight months."

He laughed. "No. Look. See how much I've filled out?" He flexed his biceps and I saw he had on the Garfield High School Football t-shirt and shorts he'd worn when he was a senior. The shirt slid up to show his abs as the poor jersey material literally strained to stay in one piece, the sleeves about to rip at the seams. And the shorts were just comical, hitting him mid-thigh and super tight.

"I'd say those are ready for the Goodwill pile," I commented, knowing that'd get a rise out of him.

"These are a piece of history, On! No way would I ever give them away!"

I chuckled. "I'm kidding. But you'd better take them off before history falls apart."

He spun to go back to his room, hollering from the hallway, "You're coming to the game today, right?"

Oh, gosh. I hadn't even thought of going, and I really didn't want to see Drake either. But when Vic came back in the kitchen—dressed in a t-shirt and shorts that actually fit—he was so excited that I couldn't say no.

"I haven't played since high school. I can't wait to put the hurt on someone," he said as he shoved a big forkful of mashed potatoes into his mouth.

"I thought it was flag?" I pointed out.

"Yeah, but you get a bunch of cocky bastards together, someone's bound to get hurt. That's what makes it fun." He snorted.

"Guys are so weird," I mumbled.

After helping with the dishes and cleaning up, he asked, "So you're going with me, yeah?"

"Yeah." I dried my hands on a towel. "You don't mind if I ask Krys to go too, do you?"

He shrugged feigning nonchalance, and I had to bite my lips to keep from laughing at the smile that graced his face, because I knew he couldn't wait to show off for her.

"Let's go," he said, grabbing his gym bag. Outside, he threw his bag in my passenger side then got on his motorcycle. "Follow me!"

When we got to the stadium, Vic was out on the field before I could even take a seat in the bleachers, and I chuckled at the way he was acting so excited like a little kid. I watched as he introduced himself to maybe twenty guys who were all freaking huge.

Drake wasn't hard to pick out sitting on the turf and stretching, his sleeveless t-shirt showing off muscular arms. I could see a tattoo on his left shoulder but couldn't make out what it was other than a tribal design. He was laughing and cutting up with two other guys which made me wonder, once again, why he was such a dick to me.

"Hey!" I heard Krystal call as she came walking up the ramp. I waved and she came up to sit by me. "These guys are hot!"

I shrugged. "You know you're only supposed to be checking out my brother."

"Oh, I will, along with the other cuties."

"He was so excited that you were coming," I informed her and got a hair flip which had me biting my lips again because from the moment she'd sat down, her eyes had followed Vic's every move.

"Hot mechanic looks hot," she mumbled.

I twisted my mouth, annoyed that she was right. "Yeah."

"Oh! He just looked up here at you!"

"Scowled is more like it," I claimed.

The game started with Drake playing quarterback on the same team as Vic, who was a receiver, and they worked great together. After Drake threw to Vic to make their third touchdown the rest of the guys started complaining, so Vic traded teams.

Now things got really interesting because Vic had been an All-State linebacker and he kept blitzing Drake who I could tell was getting agitated at being forced to run or throw quickly.

"Go Vic!" I yelled standing and clapping when on the next play, he "sacked" Drake, knocking his ass to the grass. I know. I was being a bitch. But he deserved it.

The next play, the football flew up into the bleachers almost hitting me.

"What the fuck?" I said standing and turning to look down at Krystal.

"I think you pissed him off," she stated.

I swiveled back and narrowed my eyes when I saw Drake smirking at me from the field. Ass.

"Throw the ball back, On!" Vic yelled.

I walked up two seats behind me to get the ball then gripping it, threw a perfect spiral that almost made it to where Drake stood, whose look of surprise made nearly being smoked by the ball he'd thrown worth it.

"Take that, jerkface," I mumbled walking back to sit by Krystal.

"Vic taught you well," she said with a giggle. "You see the look on hot mechanic's face?"

"Yep." I giggled right along with her.

~*~*~*~*~

Two hours later, the game ended and Krystal and I walked to the parking lot.

"Well, that was fun," she said. "I think I used up all my hot guy allowance for the month, though."

"Does that mean you're gonna have to go out with just-okay-looking thieves now? Wait. That's already happening." I rolled my eyes.

She laughed as she opened the door of her Beemer. "Well, it does keep things interesting."

"I guess so," I said with a snigger.

"I'll see you tomorrow. Tell Vic he played a good game," she said before getting in and driving off.

I walked to where I'd parked Betsy which was right at the entrance and by Vic's bike. Just before I got to her, there came Drake out of the gate. Goody.

"Loved watching you shake your pom poms," he said, all cocky as he walked by.

"You're just a…a piece of work, you know that?" I fired back. Ooooh, great comeback, I thought as I inwardly rolled my eyes at what a lame-o I was.

He turned and shot back, "I *am* a piece of work, sweetheart. Like Michelangelo's *David*, I'm that fucking amazing."

"Oh, yeah? Well, he has a tiny penis!" I announced then my eyes got big because I was shocked at what I'd said. I was also mentally high-fiving myself at my awesome retort.

That stopped him in his tracks and a couple of the guys chuckled as they walked past him. He sauntered back to me making me back up against Betsy's door.

Leaning down, his eyes glittering as they held mine, he replied, "Honey, you ever find yourself lucky enough to take my nine inches, you'll rave just like the others that my cock is a fucking masterpiece."

With that, he turned and casually strolled away getting in an older, like a 70s model, very cool, black car—Vic would've called it a muscle car—as I stood there staring after him like an idiot.

Vic called from his bike on the other side of my truck, "You coming?"

I could've made a crude comment right about then, but I restrained myself. "Uh huh," I answered instead then followed him back to the house.

CHAPTER 6

Vic texted the next Tuesday to tell me that Drake's dad had called letting him know the parts had come in and said I could bring Betsy in the next morning. I hoped it would be the last time I ever had to set foot in their garage and/or deal with Drake.

Text Message—Tues, Feb 23, 6:22 p.m

Me: This is the last time, promise

Krys: Good. I can't keep robbing banks for you. I saw my wanted poster in the post office the other day. They're onto me...

Me: Funny

Krys: So what're you promising now???

Me: Ha don't act like I always promise stuff!

Krys: Hm...Oh, Krys, I promise I'll save you a seat on the bus and you won't have to sit by someone weird!

Me: OMG That was in 6th grade! And Mrs. Price made everyone move to the back and double up!

Krys: Well, YOU didn't have to sit next to Tyler Weir(do) who used to chase us around the gym with his big old chapped lips with that weird habit of opening his mouth wide 30 billion times a day because he said it made them feel better

Me: LMAO I can't help it if you were late! And Tyler Weir was kinda cute

Krys: CUTE? They're all cute until they hold you down and try to smear their ChapStick on your mouth!

Me: Aw! It was because he liked you!

Krys: You're so mean!

Me: I'm dying hahahahaha

Krys: I hate you

Me: You love me 'cause I make you awesome snacks

Krys: Wellllll

Me: Like the dirt cake I'm gonna make you tonight

Krys: OMG OREOS

Me: Yep!

Krys: WHIPPED CREAM

Me: GUMMY WORMS

Krys: YUMMY! So what's the dealio?

Me: I need a ride in the morning from Powers to class then to work after PLEASEEEEE

Krys: Psh that's easy. And jsyk, I'd do just about anything for dirt pudding

Me: That's what I was hoping for. Thank you! You're the best EVER!

Krys: I know ;)

Me: You are. I owe you!

Krys: Nah. Just keep appeasing my sweet tooth & we're even

Me: Thank you so much, Krys, really

Krys: No problem! See you in the morning. Oh, will Mr. 9-Incher be there?

*Me: Probably *eye roll**

Krys: If he is, we'll put his gorgeous ass on ignore

Me: I can do that

Krys: K see you tomorrow!

~*~*~*~*~

"Should be ready Friday," Matt Powers said typing into the computer from behind the counter. He looked at the computer screen reading something.

"Thanks," I replied, looking cautiously around the shop for Drake. When I didn't see him, I sighed in relief then had to silently berate myself for hoping he was in the garage trapped underneath a car.

Matt went out to the garage, and I now sat in the service area alone waiting on Krystal who'd texted saying she was running late. I was flipping through a *People* magazine when I saw Drake's black muscle car come pulling into the lot. Yippee.

I set the magazine back on the table watching as he got out looking hotter than ever, dang it. His low-slung jeans and denim shirt over a white tank tee, hair still damp from his shower, and that damned cocky swagger he had as he walked toward the garage had me mesmerized. But when a white Porsche 911 came flying into the lot, stopping and a gorgeous blonde who looked like a model got out, the look-there's-a-hot-guy-within-one-hundred-yards-of-you spell I'd been under was instantly broken. And when she began yelling at him I really snapped out of it. Whoa.

"I just want a chance! It's not fair!" the woman screeched, stomping her stilettoed foot in the tight jeans she wore along with a shimmery peach-colored blouse under what I figured was a real white mink coat.

Crap. I realized I was watching a lover's quarrel play out right before my very voyeuristic eyes but found I couldn't *not* watch. Ergh.

I heard Drake reply, but unable to make out what he said, my nosy self leaned forward, and I turned my head slightly to the side to help me hear better. Then watching as he crossed his arms over his broad chest and glared at her, I felt kind of bad for the chick because I'd been on the receiving end of that look from him before and it hadn't been fun.

"It wasn't enough!" she shrieked with another foot stomp.

I sat back in my seat now rolling my eyes because I guessed nine-inch lover boy had failed to leave her raving about his masterpiece the night before. Whatever.

When he suddenly turned and headed toward the door, my body gave a surprised jolt and I grabbed the magazine again, holding it in front of my face acting as if I hadn't been watching them. Shit. The door opened making the sound of the chick peeling out of the lot loud and I heard him snort.

Don't see me. Don't see me. Don't see me, I silently prayed scooting down in the chair and trying to become invisible.

"Get a good show?" Drake asked.

I looked up innocently from the magazine. "Huh? Oh, I was just reading about Ryan Reynolds being the sexiest dad alive."

With narrowed eyes, he walked over to where I sat then taking the magazine out of my hands, flipped it right side up and handed it back.

I felt my face get hot as I chewed the inside of my lip watching him walk behind the counter. "Whoops."

"Yeah. Whoops," he mumbled as he started typing on the keyboard. Then he glanced up at me. "Why the scrubs?"

I looked down at the maroon scrubs I wore and in the process of opening my mouth to explain saw Krystal pull up. "My ride's here! Gotta go!" I declared, standing and grabbing my bag, making my way the heck out of there pronto.

"Sorry I was late!" Krystal said when I got in her car.

"It's okay. You got here just in time to keep me from making a bigger fool of myself," I answered, proceeding to tell her about the magazine debacle.

She cracked up. "Oh, On, you are just the cutest!"

"Adorable," I muttered.

~*~*~*~*~

Vic picked me up then dropped me off at home after I'd gotten off work that evening before he headed to work himself. An hour later, Krystal came over so she could eat some of her dirt cake.

"And Mrs. Johnson called me an idiot today because 'Robert' apparently hasn't been taking any of my calls," I relayed to her about how work had gone. I opened the fridge door and grabbed the cake, but when I put it on the counter and took off the cover, I was pissed. "Son of a bitch!"

"What?" she asked coming over to see what the problem was.

"I'm gonna kill my brother," I hissed seeing that he'd eaten half the cake, which I'd told him not to touch.

Krystal laughed. "It's okay. And my hips thank him."

I prepared both of us a plate and we sat in the living room while a mindless reality TV show played in the background.

"So I have another date tomorrow night," she shared. I raised my eyebrows. "This guy is the son of one of Mom's friends."

"Oh, boy. So they both have you already married, huh? And when it doesn't work out, their friendship will be ripped apart when they each blame the other's kid for it not working," I declared.

"Wow, how very optimistic of you."

I laughed. "Sorry. That was pretty crappy of me to say."

"Nah. You're probably not far off." She giggled. "Remember me telling you about Tim from the vacation our families took together right before senior year in high school? I told you I was pretty sure he was gay."

"Wait. Is this the guy you said kept critiquing your lipstick?"

"Yes! I had on Trendy Mauve one day and he told me that Posh Pink would look better with my skin tone." She laughed.

"Well, if he's not gay, at least he'll keep you looking good," I said with a chuckle. As she took a bite of her cake, I questioned, "Why do you keep going out with these guys?"

She shrugged. "I don't know. I guess it's better than not having anything to do. Plus, like I told you before, it's kinda fun meeting new people."

I so wanted her and Vic to get back together and just as I opened my mouth to say something, she stopped me. "Don't, On." Dang, she knew me so well. "Look, if it's meant to be, it will be. If not, then so be it. In the meantime, he can keep banging every skank this side of the Mississippi and I'll keep going out on bad dates."

Well, all right then.

"I know. I just…" I began, but getting a hair flip and then seeing her face, I conceded. "Shutting up now."

We finished eating our cake not talking about anything too serious, laughing and rolling our eyes at the family on TV that was having yet another "crisis" over something ridiculous.

"Pick you up in the morning," she said, giving me a hug before leaving.

~*~*~*~*~

I almost stayed home from school again Friday not wanting to bother for rides, but Jeremiah had called the night before and when I'd mentioned skipping, he'd offered to take me to school and then work, so I went with it, telling him I'd pay for his gas so I didn't feel as if I owed him anything. After picking me up for class, he'd stopped to fill up on gas, gladly letting me pay the almost fifty bucks for his full tank, which I knew was way too much for just two rides, but whatever. After work, Victor was there and took me to get Betsy.

When we pulled up, Betsy was sitting outside and through the service area window, I saw Drake behind the counter. When he heard Vic's bike, he turned and gave my brother a chin raise at which Vic nodded and I rolled my eyes at their cool-guy hello.

"You don't need me to go in and hold your hand again, do ya?" Vic asked with a snort as I handed him my helmet.

I frowned. "No."

"Good 'cause I really need to get to work," he said, raising his brow making sure I'd be okay.

"I'm fine. Go. Hopefully, this'll be the last time I have to come here."

"Yeah. Okay, see ya tomorrow."

"Love you!" I hollered just as he roared off then blowing out a breath, I turned to go inside. Drake, of course, was his usual warm and fuzzy self, giving me an indifferent look. "I'm here to pick up my truck."

I thought I heard him mumble, "No shit," but I let it go. This would be the last time I had to see him anyway so no need to get into it with him and threaten to call the Better Business Bureau.

"Three-nineteen-fifty," he said after tapping on the keyboard. I handed him my debit card and our fingers accidentally brushed when he took it causing him to scowl at me.

Good grief.

Of course, not listening to my inner voice that was chanting, "Ignore! Ignore!" I couldn't keep my big mouth shut.

"What's your problem with me, anyway?" I snapped.

His callous eyes hit mine. "Wasn't aware that I had a problem."

I shook my head in disbelief but kept quiet, just wanting to leave. After signing the receipt, I snatched up my keys that he'd placed on the counter.

"Thanks," I said walking to the door. "See ya never," I mumbled as I went out and got in my truck.

The engine started right away and as I backed out, this time when Drake turned to look at me, I temporarily lost any class I had and gave him the bird and saw the side of his mouth twitch. Ass.

"Goodbye and good riddance," I said just as I pulled up to exit the lot.

Annnnd just as I got to the road to turn and leave, Betsy died.

"No!" I yelled, trying to start her again...and again...and yet again. When she didn't fire up, I screamed, "Oh, my God!" throwing my head back against the headrest.

I was what Vic called an angry crier meaning, when I got frustrated or mad, I sometimes lost it because normally, I wasn't a huge crier. And right then, I was having to seriously hold my shit together because I was beyond pissed. So after a moment of deep breathing where I tried to find my Zen, I got out—slamming the door—and stomped back to the shop. Pulling on the door, I found it was locked, so banging on it with my fist I watched as Drake came out of the garage, an annoyed frown on his face as he came to the door, unlocking it and pushing it open for me.

"What now?" he asked, clearly agitated.

And here came the tears, damn it.

"What now? What now is my truck died again! I'm so sick of this! I can't keep having people give me rides all the time! I need her fixed now!" I shared—none too gracefully—through my tears.

The way he looked, panicked at my crying, was almost comical, and I would've laughed had I not been so upset. But I was upset, so at that moment there was nothing funny about it at all. He promptly grabbed a flashlight then yanking his jacket from a hook on the wall, pulled it on as he walked out into the parking lot with me following behind.

He was all business now, no smartassed comments or telling me what to do as he took charge—which would've been sexy had I noticed. He popped the hood with the lever from inside my truck then went to the front and pushed it up. I watched as he looked around the engine moving the light and checking things with his hands, producing a wrench from his jacket pocket and loosening what I thought was the battery cables. He inspected the ends then put them back on. He next got inside my truck and tried starting it. When nothing happened, he got back out, moving to the engine again to take another look.

"Goddamn it," he muttered, jerking on something to where part of his combed-back hair fell onto his forehead which would've been hot, but, yeah, again, I was too upset to pay attention. "Fucking Titus," he bit out as he stood then glanced down at me, actually seeming remorseful. "I think the fuel pump ground wire might've come loose."

Well, that explained it. Riiiiight.

Gazing at me for a moment, he asked, "Can you steer it if I push your truck to the garage?" I nodded and went to get in the cab. "Put it in neutral," he called. I did as I was told, then he moved to the front and closing the hood, started pushing Betsy back into the lot. "Turn her!" he yelled, which I did, turning the steering wheel so I was now facing the shop. He next walked to the back of the truck and again pushed so that I was then headed for one of the garage bays. "Brake!" he shouted as we got close to one of the doors that was down, which, duh, I'd already put my foot on the brake to stop.

I got out and asked hopefully, "Can you fix it now?"

He shook his head. "I'll have to look at it." At my disappointed expression, he apologized. "Sorry."

Huh. The great Drake Powers was actually being nice. Would wonders never cease.

"It's okay," I mumbled since it seemed he'd done everything he could.

"You need a ride?" he questioned as we walked to the service area door.

"No, I'll call my boyfriend to pick me up," I blurted pulling out my phone.

Okay, that just came out. I'd meant to say my best friend, but now I had to go with it. Crap.

Mentioning Jeremiah was kind of a dick move on my part because—

A. I didn't think of him as my boyfriend.

B. Maybe I'd said it because I didn't want Drake to think I was as pathetic as I appeared after crying about having to get rides.

And C. I kind of wanted to see his reaction.

And he did react. An expression—other than the usual irritation or cockiness he always exhibited when it came to me—appeared on his face. Surprise, maybe?

"What?" I inquired, frowning yet again. Jeez. I frowned so much around this guy I was going to have premature wrinkles.

He shrugged as he pulled a pack of cigarettes from his jacket pocket, lighting one then holding the pack out to me, which I waved off before taking a few steps away and turning my back to him where I called

Krystal first, who hadn't answered, damn it, so I got Jeremiah who said he'd be there in five minutes.

After hanging up, I walked back to Drake who smirked as he took a few more puffs of his cigarette then opened and held the door for me to go inside.

It was at that moment my brain decided to catch up, and his reaction to my boyfriend comment became clear making me frown, of course. "You think I can't get a boyfriend," I declared haughtily.

He tipped his head back and barked out a laugh, which would've been damned attractive had he not been such a prick. Then flicking his cigarette out into the parking lot, he swept the same hand faux-gallantly toward the inside of the shop for me to go in.

"You're *such* a jerk," I hissed, passing him as I went in to wait for Jeremiah.

Sooner than I knew what was going on, Drake grabbed me by the upper arm, spinning me to face him, bending to get right in my face. "I think you're fucking beautiful." His eyes burned into mine—which were now huge at his shocking declaration. "And you haven't even told me your fucking name," he rumbled letting my arm go.

My hair was in a messy bun and I still had on the well-worn UDub hoodie and old faded jeans I'd put on that morning, so no way was I looking beautiful, and I stood in confusion staring as he walked behind the desk. Leaning down he started typing, probably making out a work order for Betsy, and I could tell he was agitated by the way his fingers pounded the keys.

"It's Honor," I offered, my eyes warily on him because what in the world was going on?

"I know," he answered, pecking away at the keyboard.

"But you said—" I started.

He looked up and interrupted, "I said *you* didn't tell me your name."

I jerked my head back. So he'd been pissy to me this entire time because I hadn't made a proper introduction? God. I couldn't figure this guy out.

Just then Jeremiah pulled up and honked.

Looking out the window, I informed, "That's my, uh...Jeremiah. Um, do you know when Betsy will be ready?"

Drake stood tall now, an amused look on his face. "Betsy?"

I felt my face get hot and explained, "My truck."

He grinned. "*Betsy'll* be ready tomorrow." He looked down at the computer then back at me. "Looks like we've only got your brother's number here. Give me yours so I can call and let you know when she's ready."

I knew it was stupid, but I felt a thrill run through me that he wanted my number. Then I chastised myself inside my ridiculous head because he only wanted it for business purposes. Duh.

I gave him my number then thanked him and had nearly gotten to the door to leave when he said low, "It were me, I wouldn't sit in the fucking parking lot honking. I'd come in and get you. Ask the mechanic what was up with the truck."

I turned back to him to see his eyes intense on mine again.

"No. Actually, I'd fix the fucker for you, or at least pick it up and bring it to you so you wouldn't have to. Also wouldn't have you getting stranded by yourself in a bad part of town in front of a fucking low-grade strip club known for selling drugs," he went on.

Oh. So that's where Betsy had broken down last week. That explained the shady people. Yikes.

"Okay," I whispered because I had no idea what else to say. I wasn't sure if he was implying he wanted to date me—yeah, because he'd been so nice to me up until then ha!—and I was a bit intimidated by him right then.

"But that's just me, Honor."

I liked how my name sounded coming off his lips. Which reminded me. "You didn't introduce yourself either."

I watched as the left side of his mouth tipped up. "Drake Powers."

God, he was handsome. I bit the inside of my lip then stated, "It's nice meeting you, Drake."

Jeremiah honked again and I looked out at his truck then turned back to Drake.

"Go. I'll call you tomorrow," he said, his golden eyes now darker as they bore into mine.

"Okay. Thank you again," I replied, hesitating a moment before going out the door.

Getting into Jeremiah's truck, I gave him a *Hi*, then turning to grab my seatbelt caught Drake still watching me from inside the shop.

Our eyes stayed glued to each other's as Jeremiah and I drove off.

CHAPTER 7

"Can I come in?" Jeremiah asked when we pulled up at the curb in front of my house.

"I have to study for a test," I lied.

I really shouldn't have called him because now it felt as if I was just using him, which I guessed I was. Crap.

In the four months we'd been "seeing" each other, Jeremiah and I had barely even made it to first base and I didn't plan on ever letting him hit a homerun either. We'd kissed exactly once which had been more a peck than a kiss and had resulted when I'd turned my head to him and he'd been right there, and just went for it before I could push him away. We'd met at a party given by mutual friends and had kind of bonded over a game of beer pong when we'd ended up on the same team. And that's about as far as our bonding had gone, at least for me, seeing that he worked at a fast-food joint and had no aspirations of ever doing anything else. So even though I thought I'd made it pretty plain that I wasn't interested in anything serious, he just kept sticking around, asking me to go to movies and the like. I'd gone out with him a couple times explaining it was solely as friends, making sure to pay for myself, but on our last "date," he'd made it evident he wanted more. I'd restated my position on our relationship but I saw now he still thought I might change my mind. That wasn't going to happen because there was something about him that I didn't quite trust, something a little strange just under the surface, but I couldn't put my finger on it. Krystal felt the same and never missed a chance to remind me he was going nowhere in life if his only goal for it was, in her words, to ask, "You want fries with that?"

"You have to study for a test…" he murmured. "It's Friday, Honor. When's your test?" The look he gave me told me he totally knew I was lying.

"Monday," I kept up my fib. "But it's gonna be hard so I need to get a start on it."

He sighed. "Guess I should just give up then, huh?"

I turned in the seat to face him. "I'm sorry. You're a nice guy, Jeremiah. It's just that I don't have time for a relationship right now," I explained, trying to let him down easy yet again.

"This is fucked up," he unexpectedly spit out, glaring at me murderously.

Yikes. Well, he *had* been a nice guy.

My hand went to the door handle and I got out of there fast, throwing a ten onto the passenger seat and tossing out an apology as I closed the door. As I headed to the front porch, he yelled out the window, "Don't call me again, you fucking bitch!" spinning his tires as he left.

Well, there you go. I'd known there was something he'd been hiding—he was secretly a douche.

Just as I got inside, my phone rang.

"Hey, I saw you called. Sorry, I was at yoga," Krystal said after I answered.

"Yeah. It's okay. Betsy broke down again but I got a ride from Jeremiah, who just proved he really is a dick."

"How so?" When I told her what he'd hollered at me, she proclaimed, "Nice. See? I knew he was a weirdo *and* a stage-five clinger!"

I chuckled. "Dodged that bullet, didn't I?"

"Most definitely did."

But I felt there was a bigger gun aimed my way with a much bigger bullet when I thought of how Drake had looked at me earlier tonight.

Oh, boy.

~*~*~*~*~

"Hello?" I answered my phone Saturday evening at five as Krystal and I drove home from a day of shopping.

She'd called that morning saying she needed a new dress for the date with Tim she'd made for the next afternoon—which she figured would be a disaster as usual, but she still wanted to look good in case he tried critiquing her again. I'd laughed and agreed to go, although I abhorred shopping, but I knew I owed her since she'd given me so many rides lately. Plus, there was the fact that she was my bestie and I'd do anything for her. After shopping, we'd had lunch and seen a movie which had made up for a morning of having to visit thirty different stores before she found the perfect dress...back at the first store we'd visited. Fun.

I'd also made her more brownies and planned on giving them to her when we got to my house, but I told her I needed to do more to pay her back, at which she accused me of trying to make her fat. We'd been laughing about that being my master plan when my phone had rung with a number I didn't know.

"Hey, beautiful," Drake replied.

I blushed for a moment then bit the inside of my lip thinking he'd sure changed his tune from how he'd treated me up until I'd said Jeremiah was my boyfriend. Hm. That's when he'd started being nice.

Note to self: Must ask Krys about this.

"Hey," I said shyly. Clearing my throat, I asked, "Is Bets—er, my truck ready?"

"It's him, isn't it?" Krystal said—loudly.

"Shh!" I shushed, covering the mouthpiece on my phone.

I'd told her that morning what he'd said the night before and she'd gotten all giddy, which, apparently, her giddiness was resurfacing.

I heard his deep chuckle and rolled my eyes at her.

"Yeah. I'm bringing it to you. Need your address," he said.

I gave Krystal a panicked look and covering my phone again, whisper-hissed, "He wants my address! What do I do?"

She gave me a *duh* face. "Give it to him!"

"Uh, you don't have to do that," I told him, looking at Krystal, eyebrows raised in question. "I can come and pick it up."

She frowned and shook her head. "Let him bring it!"

I bugged my eyes out at her at how loud she was being. God.

"Gimme your address," he ordered bossily.

I now narrowed my eyes at her when she smiled great big as I told him where I lived.

"See you in twenty," he announced and hung up.

"Oh, my God! Now I get to see Mr. Badass Mechanic guy up close and personal!" she chirped as she pulled into my drive. "*And* eat more brownies!" She was out of the car in a flash, dancing on her black high-heeled boots to the front door as her pink, trendy shawl fluttered behind her, making her look like Rapunzel with her flowing long, blond hair as she crowed, "Best. Day. Ever!"

I snorted at how silly she was, loving that she could be so carefree. I worried about her career choice, though. She was going into pediatric oncology, and although I knew the kids would love her and she them, I just hoped being around those precious, ailing children wouldn't break her spirit.

Grabbing my purse, I followed her inside the house, she had her own key, and found her in the kitchen already snarfing down a brownie.

"Omigod, these are so freaking good!" she said with a moan, grabbing for a second one.

"This time I added honey," I revealed smiling as she literally inhaled the treats.

"You're a baking goddess," she returned, mouth full as she opened the fridge to pour herself a glass of milk.

"I need to ask you if you think Drake's only being nice to me because of Jeremiah, and now this has become some kind of weird competition thing?"

She twisted her mouth in thought—or more to get the sticky brownie out of her teeth—before taking a drink. "Maybe. Or it could've made him see you differently or something, you know?" She split another brownie in two, popping half into her mouth. "Wanna know the truth?" she garbled.

"Nope. Lie to me."

She chuckled as she swallowed, bringing the glass up ready to take a drink. "I think it was your crying that got to hi—" She froze, glass halfway to her mouth.

"What's all the commotion," Vic interrupted, coming into the kitchen.

Spotting Krystal, he went rigid too, staring at her as if he was seeing a ghost. My eyes were the only things not suspended in time as they moved back and forth between the two of them as if they were playing a tennis match. As far as I knew, this was the first time they'd been together in the same room since breaking up.

Shit.

"I thought you were at work. I didn't see your motorcycle," I whispered breaking the silence.

He replied quietly, his eyes staying on Krystal, "Night off. I parked it out back."

"Oh." What else could I say. Eep!

"I've gotta go," Krystal said abruptly, setting her glass down on the counter before flipping her hair behind her shoulder showing she was annoyed.

"No!" I all but yelled, making them both jump, surprising even myself with my outburst. "You're not going anywhere. I need you here. Remember?" I canted my head to the side, raising my eyebrows in an attempt to remind her that Drake was coming by.

"Stay." Vic's eyes were intense as he gazed at her. Then he looked at me. "I've gotta go anyway." Turning on his boot heel he headed to the front door where he grabbed one of his many leather jackets off a hook and went out the door.

I looked back at Krystal. "You okay?"

She nodded distractedly, picking her glass back up and taking a long drink. Then the hair flipping was all over the place. "I'm good." *Flip.* "I just hate..." *Flip.* "that he's still..." *Flip* "so hot..." *Flip.*

I heard voices outside and knew Drake must've arrived and was probably talking to Vic.

"Come on. I need to get the keys from him and pay," I said, going to my purse on the counter and digging around for my checkbook as Krystal scooted out of the kitchen with an excited squeal.

She was peeking through the curtains out the front window when I got into the living room. "It's like a hot guy convention out there," she said in awe, keeping her voice low.

I went to stand next to her and saw Vic talking to Drake along with another guy who looked a lot like Drake but younger and not as big. "Must be one of his brothers," I said perfunctorily, because I only had eyes for Drake. My God, he was beautiful.

The guys laughed about something then suddenly all three happened to look right at us, you know, we girls who were gaping at them from the window.

Krystal quickly let the curtain go and we both stepped back.

"You think they saw us?" she gasped, her eyes big.

"Not a chance," I responded, huffing out a snicker as I walked to the door because of course they saw us. Duh.

"Wait for me!" she said, her heels clicking on the wood floor as she hurried to catch up.

Going out onto the porch, I heard Vic's bike start then he zoomed off past my truck that was parked in the drive, throwing his left hand down in that cool biker acknowledgment, pointer and middle fingers together, basically saying goodbye. I looked back to see Drake ascending the steps but he stopped when he saw me, his eyes traveling over my body, and making my face get hot.

"No scrubs or hoodie tonight?" he asked, his sexy lips twitching as he and the guy—who seeing him up close I knew *had* to be his brother—both came on up to stand on the porch.

From over my shoulder, Krystal answered, "No! We went shopping today because she didn't have to work!"

"Yeah?" he inquired of her then gazed down at me. "Where do you work?"

"She works at Colonial Manor. It's a nursing home. And she recently got her license so she can give out meds!" Krystal shared, apparently embracing wholeheartedly the role of being my personal herald.

"I like the jeans," Drake announced.

Krystal jumped in again. "Aren't they cute? I got them for her on her last birthday! They're True Religion! And they make her butt look amazing! See?" She grabbed me by the shoulders spinning me to face her.

Oh. My. God.

I swatted her hands off of me and quickly turned back to face Drake who was smirking. The guy off to his side donned a similar expression.

Kill me now.

"Ignore my friend. She's obviously delusional," I muttered, mortified that I'd been subjected to that ridiculous display of...my ass. God.

"Oh! I'm Krystal. You must be Drake," she now said, holding out her hand to shake his. She looked at the other guy. "And you're his brother?"

"Titus," the guy said with a nod, shaking her hand and snorting at her boldness. He held his hand out to me next. "Nice meeting you, Honor." He winked at me as if he knew some big secret which had me jerking my head back wondering what the heck that was all about.

I looked at Drake. "Thank you for bringing Bets—I mean, my truck back. She's good now?"

He nodded, grinning as he reached into his jeans pocket and pulled out the keys. "Good as new," he said, holding them out to me.

"Really, thank you so much," I replied. "What do I owe you?" I opened my checkbook and took the pen ready to write the check.

"No charge."

My head snapped up. "What? No, we can't do this again!"

His half smirk let me know he'd been ready for my response. Well, that and the way he glanced at his brother like, *I told you the crazy chick would protest*.

That's when Titus stepped in. "This was my fault." At my questioning look, he shared. "I worked on it."

He left that hanging there as if it explained everything. Good grief. He talked just like his brother.

I found myself on repeat of what I'd said to Drake the other night. "And?"

Titus grinned sheepishly. "I must've knocked loose the ground wire." He shrugged. "That's why it wouldn't start."

Ah. That was a better explanation.

"But what about labor?" I asked, not wanting something for nothing from them yet again.

Titus looked at Drake and chuckled.

Now what?

"Took what, twenty minutes, tops?" he asked.

Drake nodded then looked at me. "You really wanna pay?"

I glanced at Krystal who'd fallen silent then back at him. "Well, yeah."

"You serious about the guy who picked you up last night?" he queried.

My brow dipped. "Jeremiah? Um, no."

He actually smiled then. "Good. Tomorrow. Seven. I'll pick you up."

Looking at Titus, Drake jerked his head toward the black muscle car I'd just noticed sitting in the street. Then both guys turned and descended the porch steps walking toward it.

"Wait!" I called, going down the steps after him. He stopped walking, nodding at Titus to keep going before turning to face me. "Why're you being so nice to me all of a sudden?" I asked, eyes narrowed.

He chuckled. "I wasn't being nice before?"

"Well, no."

"Huh."

"It's not because I said I have a boyfriend, is it?" I questioned.

"Babe."

There was that way he talked. When he said nothing else, I said, "What?"

He let out a breath as his eyes went soft and golden. "Guess I finally opened up my eyes and saw what was in front of me."

I bit the inside of my lip at how sweet he was being. "Oh."

"Yeah." He turned when Titus started the car then looked back at me, ordering, "Tomorrow. Seven." Annnd Mr. Confident was back.

"What if I'm not free?" I postured, only a tiny bit snottily. FYI—I was *so* free it wasn't even funny but his cocky self didn't need to know that.

"Get free," he advised.

"But—"

He reached out a hand pushing my hair behind my shoulder then held my neck at the back. Leaning down and getting right in my face, his eyes danced in amusement as if he knew I had no plans. Our noses were nearly touching, our lips a mere inch apart which made me suck in a breath before he said, "Get free, babe."

"Okay," I whispered because damn.

I saw his eyes crinkle at the sides when he echoed, "Okay." He pulled back and muttered, "*Really* like those jeans," then walked away, got in the car with Titus and they drove off.

"You are in so much trouble," I proclaimed to myself as I turned and went back to the porch where Krystal waited grinning big.

CHAPTER 8

Maybe I hadn't lied to Jeremiah about not having time for a relationship if the hours it had taken to even choose a freaking outfit for my date the next night meant anything.

"Pink is your color, not mine," I whined to Krystal, whose date with Tim had taken place that afternoon.

It was Sunday, I'd no sooner gotten home from work than I'd jumped in the shower, and my date with Drake loomed within the hour. Ack! Krystal had been waiting for me when I'd gotten out and was now helping me dress having already done my hair and makeup in record time.

"But you look pretty!" she confirmed.

I looked in the mirror seeing that the pink voile button-up blouse over a white camisole she'd chosen from my closet actually appeared to look quite good together. Canting my head to the side, I examined my black skinny jeans and the sexy pink stilettos I'd borrowed from her that finished the ensemble.

"Okay. It's not that bad," I admitted.

She puffed out a laugh. "Not bad? You look great!" She twisted one of my curls between her fingers then grabbed the eyebrow pencil using the brush end to shape my brows one last time, getting everything "just so." She stepped back scrutinizing me. "If this doesn't get you laid, I give up."

"What?" I burst out. "That's not the plan for tonight!"

She giggled. "I know." Then she cut her eyes at me. "But still."

"So today was bad?" I asked.

"*So* bad at the beginning. First, he let me know he knew my 'Manolo Blahniks' were knockoffs. I mean, what man knows that who isn't gay? And second, he told me my eyeshadow should be more taupe than brown." She raised an eyebrow. "So I flat-out asked him if he was gay."

My mouth dropped open. "You did not."

She nodded. "His response? 'Girl, I'm a giant homo.'" We both cracked up. "He's the coolest guy ever. Best date I've been on in a while."

"Good!" I replied. "You needed a fun date."

"He said he's told his parents but they don't believe him. But his boyfriend understands that he occasionally has to go out with whomever they hook him up with." She giggled. "I think we might hang out next weekend."

The doorbell rang and I felt my heart in my throat.

"Ready?" she asked, her shoulders coming up in excitement as she grinned.

I swallowed roughly and nodded. This would either go great or straight to hell. With the way Drake and I had started out, it was no doubt a toss-up.

~*~*~*~*~

Okay, *I* was going straight to hell.

Don't get me wrong. The date had been amazing so far. Drake had taken me to a really cool Italian restaurant that had tarot card readers and trapeze artists. I'll just say that again—*trapeze artists*! The atmosphere was so cool and everything going on all around us had been incredible.

After dinner, we'd gone to a bar where several live bands were playing, and they were really good! I mean, it *was* Seattle from where many great bands had originated, so I was guessing the standards for performances were pretty dang high, and the bands hadn't disappointed. And that's where we were now.

We sat in a spot toward the back where the music wasn't too loud and we could talk, continuing to keep the conversation light as we had at dinner where we'd found out we were both born and raised in Seattle. We shared a bit about our growing up, discovered we both liked the Foo Fighters—I mean, who doesn't—and talked about what we wanted for our futures. He'd told me he'd played football in college for three years but had to drop out after his junior year—when I asked where he played and the reason he'd dropped out, he'd changed the subject—but he also informed me that he'd been taking online courses to get his business degree. His goal was to open another Powers Automotive and manage both, since he'd already been doing so at the current one. He also explained that he owned a house in a neighborhood near the shop, which made it convenient for him to keep up with things.

I was now telling him about working at the nursing home explaining how Mrs. Johnson critiqued me daily and how I loved spunky, ninety-five-year-old Mr. Avery.

"He's amazing," I declared. "I hope I'm that energetic when I'm his age."

"I'm not that energetic now," Drake quipped, laughing, a before-unseen dimple appearing in his right cheek when he smiled.

Damn.

And that right there, that was the reason I was going to hell.

See, he was so fricking handsome, just so *gah!* that as we talked, all I could think about was what he would be like in bed.

Did he make sexy groans?

Did he talk dirty—I would've bet money on it.

Did he have a signature move?

Did he have a big—"Sorry, what did you say?" I asked when he spoke, my eyes moving from his dimple to his.

"I said I'll be lucky to make it to seventy," he stated with a grin.

Yep. Definitely going to hell.

As he started telling me about one of his brothers messing with him by making him late to class when they were in high school, I couldn't stop staring. He was so sexy in his dark jeans, tucked in navy button down shirt, brown tweed blazer and brown wingtip boots; his hair in its fade cut, the top a little long and combed back, and then there was the stubble on his sharp jaw that I wanted to touch, well, it amongst other things.

Holy smokes, he was hot.

So who could blame me for having yummy thoughts about him?

"I had to beat the shit out of him because he'd hidden my keys and you keep looking at me that way I'm gonna fuck you right here on the table." Drake had been in the middle of his story but I guess I'd zoned out and had been brazenly staring at his lips as they moved.

Their stopping brought me out of my reverie. "Pardon?"

The way his eyes were glittering meant he'd said something dirty, I figured. And when I finally realized what he'd just uttered, my face got hot.

"Oh," I murmured, licking my lips.

"Let's get out of here," he stated.

He stood, taking my hand and helping me off my barstool and as we made our way out, I melted at the feel of his palm on my lower back. At his black car, which I'd learned was a 1970 Chevelle SS, he unlocked my door helping me in, and while he walked around to his side, I kept my eyes on him thinking about how he'd been a gentleman the entire evening, sweet even, and obviously more attentive to the conversation than I'd been. He'd asked questions but hadn't pried and made me laugh with his comments.

Damn. He was the whole package. But I still wondered why he'd been such a jerk to me when we first met, so as we drove home, I decided to find out.

"Can I ask you a question?"

"Depends," he answered.

"Oh," I murmured kind of taken aback. He'd been so open earlier that this took me off guard.

He reached over and grabbed my hand with a chuckle. "Ask, Honor."

"Oh. Well, I was wondering why, you know, at first, you were kind of…"

He squeezed my hand before letting it go to shift as we approached a stoplight.

"Harsh?" I bit my lips trying to think of how to proceed.

"Babe, I've got a lot on my plate. You stick around, you'll see that. I was so fucking attracted to you from the start," he turned and winked before taking off when the light turned green, "but I have to be careful about who I let in my life."

I nodded but didn't really understand what he'd meant.

I guessed I'd just have to stick around and find out.

~*~*~*~*~*~

"Fuck," Drake groaned after pulling away from kissing me at my front door.

He'd walked me up to the porch and we'd been engaged in a very steamy make-out session for the last several minutes.

And good gosh, the man could kiss.

I was tempted to ask him in. Had actually started to, then my head—in deep conflict with my body—started in, telling me it wouldn't be prudent to do so. Stupid, stupid head. But I knew I was right in listening because it seemed that sex always just complicated things.

I mean, first, I hardly knew him and I wanted to know him more. And before, when I felt I'd had sex too soon with guys—I was no expert since I'd only slept with two but whatever—I'd somehow felt cheated, as if we'd jumped from A to Z and missed out on the fun in-between stuff like flirting and figuring each other out. Secondly, I wanted those long phone talks with Drake, gradually finding out who he was a bit at a time. I wanted to see the real him. I knew if he came inside, I would've jumped his sexy ass in a heartbeat and lost out on all of that. So following my logic instead of my horny body—bad, bad, horny body—I told him thank you and goodnight and went inside.

Following the very specific orders that the moment I walk in the door I call, I dialed Krystal's number and then a barrage of questions was immediately upon me:

"How'd it go? Did you have fun? What'd you do? Did he like what you wore? What'd he wear? Were you nervous? Was *he* nervous?"

I took a breath to answer—shocked that she'd restrained herself from asking the one question I knew she really wanted to know—and, of course, she didn't disappoint.

"Did you...*DO IT*?" she burst out loudly, causing me to yank the phone away from my ear.

"No!" I replied with a laugh. "But we did make out on my porch."

"This is gonna be huge, On! He could be *the one*!" she squealed.

I snorted. "We've gone on one date, Krys. Don't have me walking down the aisle just yet."

"Never know!" she gushed.

After giving her the rest of the details of our date, I got ready for bed, washing the makeup from my face and smiling dreamily thinking of how when Drake had picked me up, he'd immediately stated, "You're beautiful." As I brushed my teeth, I heard my phone bling from my bedroom and after finishing up, I went in and plopped down on my bed grabbing my cell. And I swear, I could've starred in one of those crazy gum commercials with the huge smile I sported.

Text Message—Sat, Feb 27, 11:35 a.m.

Drake: Had a great time, beautiful

How sweet was that? I lay back on my pillow and turned out the light before replying.

Me: I did too, handsome. Thank you. I had fun :)

I blushed as I hit *Send*. Gah!

Drake: What're you wearing?

That made me laugh. Men were such visual creatures.

Me: A tank top and shorts lol

Drake: Fuck

Me: What're YOU wearing? ;)

Drake: Nada, sweetheart

Now, talk about your visuals. Good gosh. I sat staring at my phone not quite knowing what to reply.

Drake: You fall asleep?

Me: No.

Drake: When can I see you again?

I sighed, loving that he wanted to see me again.

Me: I don't work Tuesday

Drake: Be ready at 7

I chuckled at that because he was definitely decisive, my new word for *bossy*.

Me: Okay

Drake: Nothing fancy

Me: Sounds good

Drake: See you then, babe

Me: Okay, Drake. Night

I fell asleep smiling.

CHAPTER 9

Tuesday night we were at O'Leary's Sports Bar and Grill playing pool. Drake had me try a couple different beers that were pretty good and I really liked the one that had a fruity taste.

As he racked the balls for our third game, he stated, "My Uncle Jack owns this place. My brothers and I practically grew up here."

"So, you guys have been drinking awesome beer and playing pool since you were toddlers, huh?" I commented just as he pulled back his stick to break.

His back tensed as he flubbed the shot. He stood tall and turned toward me, a spark in his eyes when he challenged, "You gonna be cute?"

"Uh—" was all I got out then he was stalking toward me, setting his pool stick against the table before backing me against the wall.

Both hands on the wall at either side of my head, he leaned down and stated, "'Cause I'm all for cute, Honor. Just makes me wanna fuck you even more."

Wow.

Biting the inside of my lip, I looked up at him and not knowing what else to reply whispered, "Okay."

"Jesus," he ground out.

I watched his jaw muscles tic as he gazed down at me then sliding a hand to the base of my throat his mouth came down on mine, his tongue teasing my own, twisting, swirling with it. Breathing out a moan, I smoothed my hands over his chest and up behind his neck where I curled my fingers into his hair.

And, dang, I was completely consumed by that kiss. Totally lost in him until a man suddenly hollered, "Get a room!"

Drake pulled away and grinned down at my embarrassed face. Then looking back over his shoulder, he retorted, "Go fuck yourself!"

"Already did! Twice today!" the guy returned.

Drake snorted and now slid his hand that was at the front of my throat to the back of my neck pulling me with him as he turned toward whoever was talking to him.

"That hard up, huh?" Drake asked, moving his arm around my shoulders as we walked over.

The guy looked a lot like Drake—same honey eyes, same build—meaning, he was very good looking.

When we got to him, Drake dropped his arm from me and they executed a guy hug then pulling back he asked, "What's going on, man?"

"Picking up a check from Uncle Jack," was the reply, but the guy wasn't looking at Drake, he was checking me out, his eyes giving me the up-and-down.

Drake reached a hand back for me, taking mine and pulling me up to him. "This is Honor Justice," he introduced.

"Ryker Powers," the guy said back, giving me a half smirk as he held out his hand for me to shake. His eyes traveled over my body again before they landed on Drake and he nodded as if in approval uttering, "Happy for you."

Looking up at Drake, I saw the side of his mouth tip up. "Thanks," he replied then glanced down at me. "Ryker's my cousin. He was a champion wrestler in college."

Ryker snorted. "Champion. Yeah." He raised an eyebrow and looked down at me. "This one tell you he was an All-American quarterback?"

That was an amazing feat and I glanced up at Drake just in time to see him become embarrassed. Huh. He cut his eyes toward me. "Second team," he shared and shook his head as if that wasn't damned cool either.

"Wow," I muttered, giving him a beaming smile and felt him squeeze my hand.

He then turned back to Ryker. "Where's Frankie?"

"Some fucking play she tried talking me into going to. Thank God Dad called asking me to come here and I got out of it."

Drake chuckled gazing down to give me a wink before looking back at his cousin and saying, "Chick shit."

Ryker nodded in agreement.

I frowned because plays were awesome.

"How're things at the garage?" Ryker asked.

"Good. Gotta '68 Barracuda in for a tune-up I'd think of buying if the guy'd come down about twenty grand." Drake snorted.

Ryker laughed. "What the fuck's he asking?"

"Thirty-four."

"Mint?"

"Perfect."

Ryker whistled. "I'd give you some competition for it but Frankie would chew my ass out." He looked at me and winked, explaining, "Saving for a honeymoon."

"Think I'll call her and tell her you made an offer," Drake said with an ornery grin.

"You do that and I'll tell this one," Ryker nodded toward me, "about sophomore year in high school when you got caught sneaking out of Brianna Brown's bedroom window."

"Damn. That's some low-down shit, man," Drake replied with a chuckle.

"Hey, fuck with me, I fuck with you," Ryker fired back laughing. Then he gave me a grin. "Police were involved."

"Fuck," Drake muttered.

I giggled at their witty repartee thinking it was cool that they were close.

"Okay, gotta go find Uncle Jack and pick up a check," Ryker stated.

"Good seein' you, Ryke," Drake said, shaking his hand. "Say hi to everyone for me. I think Mom's sent cards to the family to come over in a couple Sundays. See you then?"

"Yeah. Oh, tell Will I'll bring the football Zeke signed for him," Ryker said then he looked at me and nodded. "Nice meeting you, Honor."

"You too," I answered.

"Later," Drake called as Ryker walked off. Looking down at me after his cousin left he asked, "Ready?"

"Yes."

From the coatrack by the front door, Drake grabbed my jacket holding it out for me to put on before donning his own. As he opened the door, an older man called from behind the bar, "See you on the twelfth!"

I turned to see Ryker leaning against the bar having been talking to whom I assumed was their Uncle Jack.

"Yeah, see ya!" Drake called out and held the door for me to go out. He took my hand in his as we walked to his Bronco.

"You and Ryker look so much alike," I declared. "You could pass for brothers."

"The Powers gene is strong, I guess."

I'll say. I'd met his brother Titus who was a mini-me Drake and now his cousin Ryker who was practically his clone. Jeez. If the rest of his family was this gorgeous, they could totally star in their own reality TV show and really do nothing but maybe take off their shirts. Women everywhere would go nuts.

"Who's Zeke?" I inquired. "And Will?"

"Zeke's Ryker's brother," he explained, unlocking my door and opening it for me. After closing it, he walked around and got in starting the engine. "He played football at Hallervan. Wide receiver. Got drafted to the NFL."

"Cool," I replied because it *was* very cool.

"Yeah. We're all gonna try to make a game sometime when they play the Seahawks," he said as we pulled out of the parking lot.

"That'd be awesome," I concluded, duly impressed. "And who is Will?"

"Did I tell you I played football at U-Dub?" he asked, again avoiding telling me who Will was. Hm.

"You did?" He'd told me he'd played and had gotten hurt but hadn't supplied much more information as in where or beyond what Ryker had revealed.

"Yep. Quarterback. Three years then hurt my shoulder and I was done."

I looked at him realizing I didn't even know his age. "How old are you?"

He cast a glance at me out of the corner of his eye and smiled. "Twenty-five."

"I was a junior in high school when you were a junior in college. I wish I could've seen you play." My face turned pensive at my thinking I would've loved watching him.

"Would you have been my personal cheerleader and shaken your pom poms for me?" He gave me a wink before taking a right.

I rolled my eyes at the rephrasing of his smartass comment from the football field. "Yeah, because as a badass, All-American star quarterback you so would've dated a seventeen-year-old high schooler." He laughed at that. "Besides, you probably already had your own personal cheerleader anyway." Ergh. I didn't like the thought of that.

He shrugged.

Well, shit.

And that's what I'd meant about wanting to get to know him better. Well, not really wanting to know about past girlfriends, but him in general.

"You're the same age as my brother," I divulged.

"Yeah. Vic was a bad motherfucker at football. Gable loved playing with him."

Good lord. There were so many names to keep up with.

"So your cousins are Gable, Zeke, Ryker and Will?"

"Gable, Zeke, Ryker and Loch, who's the baby."

"And your brothers are?"

"You've met Titus. Then there's Kase, Blaze, Zane and Wilder."

"Cool names. But holy crap. Does your family have any girls?" I asked.

He laughed. "My dad's sister, my Aunt Melanie, lives in Idaho and she's got two girls. But Ryker's dad and mine are brothers and run the garage together, that's why we boys are all close."

"And Will is?" I asked again.

We pulled up to the curb in front of my house and he cut the engine. Then suddenly looking wary and staring down the street, he asked, "Your brother home?"

I looked for Vic's motorcycle but didn't see it. "I don't think so but he might've parked in back."

"Call him."

I pulled my head back in question. "Why?"

"Just do it."

"But Dra—"

"Now," he ordered, and rather rudely, I thought.

"You're the bossiest person I've ever met," I griped as I got my phone out of my purse. As it rang, I asked Drake, "Can you at least tell me why you wanna know?"

"Get your brother on the fucking line," he rumbled.

Seriously?

"Hey," I said when Vic answered. "Are you home?"

"No. Why?"

"Drake wanted to kno—" I didn't finish my sentence because Drake took my phone from me. God!

"Vic? Drake. Doing great, man, thanks. What do you know about this guy Honor's been seeing?"

Was he kidding right now? He was asking my brother about Jeremiah when he could've just asked me. I glowered at him listening to his *Uh huhs* and I'd had enough. Grabbing my purse, I opened my door, got out and stomped toward the house. His rude self could keep my fricking phone for all I cared. As I got to the top of the porch steps, I heard his car door slam and as I reached out to pull on the storm door handle, I was stopped because he was there, putting a hand on it to keep me from opening it.

"What the—" I spun and looked up at him angrily. "I wanna go in now, Drake."

He stared down the street again for a moment before looking back at me.

"What's going on?" I questioned, glancing to where he'd looked.

"You gonna behave like an adult or a spoiled child?" he challenged.

Yippee. Drake the jerk was back.

My head snapped around and I took a deep breath blowing it out trying to keep from going off on him. When I wasn't so sure that was going to happen, I kept my mouth closed and just scowled up at him.

He raised an eyebrow, apparently wanting an answer.

"You're infuriating," I whispered.

"Which is it?"

I glanced up at the porch ceiling and blew out another breath, highly annoyed.

How could our awesome evening have gone to shit? And why was he back to acting this way again?

When he figured out I wasn't going to answer, he nodded toward where he'd been looking and asked, "That your boyfriend's truck down the way?"

I looked quickly back down the street and saw Jeremiah's truck sitting there. What in the world? "He's not my boyfriend, but yeah, I think it's his."

"He have friends in this neighborhood?"

I shook my head. "I don't think so."

"Stay here, Honor." He narrowed his eyes at me. "I fucking mean it," he added curtly then jogged away toward Jeremiah's truck.

Suddenly the headlights came on and the tires screeched as Jeremiah drove off before Drake even made it to him. As he passed by me, it was dark, but I was pretty sure he flipped me off.

Great.

What was weirder, though, was another car did the same thing right behind Jeremiah's truck, headlights on but they pulled out, shot a U and took off in the opposite direction.

Drake stopped to watch the second car before turning and making his way back. He walked up the porch steps and questioned, "You know what that was all about?"

I winced. "I told him the other night I didn't have time for a relationship right now." His eyebrows came up as in, *Oh, really?* and I quickly clarified, "I didn't want to hurt his feelings. But I'd told him several times before that I wasn't interested in him."

"He got a taste of you and wants more."

"We never even kissed!" I revealed. "I mean, we did once, but it was just a quick peck. But we just hung out as friends, or at least that's all I told him we'd ever be." When he stayed quiet, I continued remembering

I was still mad at him. "And you could've just asked me instead of being all dramatic, having me call Vic and not telling me why."

His eyes went hard as he replied, "I don't do drama. And I was protecting you."

I huffed out a humorless laugh. "I don't need protecting."

He nodded toward where Jeremiah had been parked. "He take it well when you broke things off?"

I bit the inside of my lip. "No. He called me a fucking bitch."

I watched as Drake's body went rigid as he breathed in through his nose, his jaw muscles bunching every few seconds like he was now the one trying to stay calm, obviously pissed at what Jeremiah called me. He finally exhaled and said, "Look, I'm not always gonna candy-coat shit. If I sense something's wrong, I'm not gonna wait until shit fucking happens. I'll take care of it right then."

I couldn't help but snort at his candy-coat remark because to my best recollection, I couldn't recall his ever doing that. Then I protested, "But you could've asked me or told me what you were thinking."

"By the time I did that, it could've been too late," he insisted.

"Too late for what?" I questioned but he just stared at me not answering. I sighed knowing that how he took what I said next was very important. "Look, Drake, I want a partner. Someone who includes me, treats me as an equal, not like I can't handle things."

There was a pause before he stated, "Sounds like you're looking for a good guy, Honor."

"I am! What's wrong with that?"

His expression went hard. "I'm not him."

My brow wrinkled as my eyes narrowed at his pronouncement.

"You seem to know what you want." He reached out and ran the backs of his fingers down the side of my face. "You like soft and sweet, I can give you that. I'm just letting you know that's not always me. And I don't know if you can handle that." He turned and started walking down the steps then looking back over his shoulder disclosed, "But when you're ready for hard and rough...give me a call."

CHAPTER 10

"I think I was just broken up with," I told Krystal after going inside the house and calling her.

"What? Why?"

I put my phone on speaker on the kitchen table as I cut myself a piece of German chocolate cake then proceeded to tell her what had happened with Jeremiah and what Drake had said.

"First of all, what a fucking creep! Jeremiah, not Drake. And that doesn't sound like a breakup to me, what Drake said, not Jeremiah pulling his shit," she concluded.

"Yeah, well, I think it does. He treated me like I was a child!"

"He was protecting you, like he said," she reasoned.

"I'm a big girl. I don't need protecting."

"With the way Jeremiah's behaved, you never know."

"I can handle him." I got up and rinsed off my plate. "Oh, and Drake kept avoiding answering when I asked who Will is."

"Maybe he doesn't feel comfortable sharing everything just yet."

"I don't know if he's the right guy for me anyway. We didn't start off on a good note. And he's just too...bossy," I concluded feeling tears sting the backs of my eyes.

Krystal laughed. "Honey, he sounds just like Victor."

I went stock-still at hearing that swiping at the tears that'd escaped because she was right. "Oh, my God. He does." I sniffed and grabbed a tissue to wipe under my eyes. "But that's the thing. I don't need another bossy man in my life."

"Vic comes off as bossy but he's being protective. It's just how he is. Drake sounds the same way. They're both...what's the word? Reactive? If you'd been with Vic tonight and he'd seen the douchebag's truck, he would've done the same. Except he would've told you to," her voice went deep as she mimicked Vic, "'Get your ass in the house and don't come out until I say so!' Am I right?"

"Shit. You are."

"And how would you have behaved?"

I thought for a second. "Probably the same, mad that he was telling me what to do, but I would've done it."

"Exactly."

"Yeah, but I trust Vic," I replied, realizing right then what the problem was. "I don't know Drake well enough yet to just randomly do what he says. And what happened tonight actually kinda scared me. He'd been so sweet up until then."

"I'm sure it did. But that's what you have to decide. Do you want to get to where you trust him and put up with his protectiveness or are you over it?"

"I need to think about this." I frowned when I asked, "Do I owe him an apology?"

"Depends on what you want, On."

"Yeah." And that was the question. What *did* I want?

"But remember, you'll be fine either way," she reminded.

"Thanks, Krys. You're the best," I whispered.

We hung up and I stared at my phone wondering what to do.

I liked Drake. I was extremely attracted to him and he'd been so nice the last few days, which made me huff out a laugh because, big whoop. He'd been nice! But at least he'd shown me that side of him before going all alpha dude on me. And if something like what happened tonight occurred again, could I deal with it? Did I want to deal with it? And what exactly had he meant by hard and rough? Was he talking just how he was? Or sex? Yikes.

As I got ready for bed, I figured that was the riddle to which I needed to find an answer. So just before I turned off my light, I texted him.

Text Message—Wed, Mar 2, 12:12 a.m.

Me: I'm sorry

I fell asleep waiting for his reply. Which never came.

~*~*~*~*~

Sundays are bipolar.

If you have something to do or your state of mind is good, they're awesome.

On the other hand, if you have nothing planned or, oh, say your text message hasn't been answered in four days, they're like getting your eyebrows threaded. It hurts and, yeah, that's about it.

Lucky me had awakened at seven that morning, and no matter how hard I tried to fall back to sleep, after thirty minutes I'd finally given up and rolled out of bed. To get my mind off everything, most of which was Drake's blatant rejection, I'd started laundry, cleaned out the kitchen cabinets and made Krystal more brownies.

Well, that had taken all of an hour and ten minutes. Yeesh.

Next, I started in on the hall closet, throwing out old coats and jackets to take to Goodwill.

Thirty minutes down.

I wanted to vacuum but didn't want to wake Vic, so I'd dustmopped around the area rug in the living room then gone outside and swept off the front porch.

A whopping forty-two minutes.

Ugh.

Going back inside, I swept and mopped the kitchen floor then folded laundry.

When I saw it was only ten-thirty, I cursed under my breath. And upon hearing a giggle coming from Vic's room I muttered an even worse curse.

I'd hoped that after seeing Krystal the other evening, Victor would surely have come to his senses, and seeing the error of his ways, would've begged her to get back together with him. At the medley of chortling I now heard coming from his room, I figured that wouldn't be happening any time too soon.

An hour later my day got even better when Vic's bedroom door opened and the expected clicking of the heels advanced toward the kitchen where I was at the sink peeling potatoes to go with the roast I'd thawed.

"Oh. Hey," a snooty voice called from the doorway.

Looking over, I saw Tiffany Green, a girl with whom I'd graduated high school and who'd also stolen my boyfriend sophomore year, standing there giving me a haughty look.

Yay.

"Hey, bitch," I answered.

Jusssst kidding.

"Hey," I muttered, continuing with my peeling.

"How's it going?" she asked.

Like she cared.

"Good."

"What're you making?"

"Roast." I rolled my eyes as I turned on the faucet then the garbage disposal, pushing the peels down the drain.

"Vic's in the shower," she hollered over the noise.

"Yeah," I stated, flipping the switch off, annoyed that she was trying to hold a conversation with me.

"So..."

I glanced at her watching as she smoothed her strawberry blond hair off her forehead then adjusted the emerald green halter top that cowled at her chest, hanging so low and wide, her breasts were practically falling out. Turning back to the sink, I started peeling carrots wishing she'd leave already.

"I'm sorry about what happened with Ben."

I snorted as I kept working. "That was five years ago."

Why these women, Tiffany included, thought schmoozing me would improve their chances with Vic, I had no idea. Maybe they were hoping I'd put in a good word for them. That would be happening never for Tiffany. Not that I gave a rat's ass that she'd stolen my high school boyfriend. It was that she wasn't a nice person, having done the same to two other girls throughout school—not that anyone can "steal" anyone per se. It's that she purposely lured the guys away just to prove that she could. She'd also been a hateful snob. *That's* why I didn't care for her.

"Yeah, but I still feel bad."

A glimpse her way showed me she was totally lying if the smirk on her face meant anything. Just as I thought. Still a hateful snob.

"Sounds like a personal problem to me," I murmured, unwrapping the roast and putting it into the pan.

"I mean, I can't help it if Ben was so easy, you know."

I stopped chopping the onion and celery and turned to her, my bad mood moving to the forefront, and told her the truth. "Oh, *Ben* was easy?" I challenged, raising my brow. "You know, it wasn't like he wanted you. He just wanted an easy fuck. He told me that later. It's what they all wanted. What they still want." I now pointed my knife at her. "My brother included."

Her mouth fell open and her eyes narrowed. "W-well, I never!" she sputtered.

"Oh, you *always*," I retorted with a giggle. Oh, my God, it felt good saying that.

"You're such a bitch! That's the reason Ben cheated on you!" she fired back.

"Ben cheated on me because he knew you'd spread your legs for him and I wouldn't," I stated matter-of-factly.

"I can't help it if you were an uptight cunt!" she declared.

I smiled knowing she was about to get told when I saw Vic round the corner.

"'The fuck you just call my sister?" he bellowed.

Tiffany turned to him in surprise. "She was—she said—"

"Leave," he said firmly.

"But I thought we—" she started.

"I need to carry your ass out of here?" he warned.

I felt kind of bad seeing her tear up as she tried mustering some decorum, having to dig pretty deep, I supposed. But she'd brought this all on herself.

As she headed to the door, she looked back at Vic and spit out, "I faked all my orgasms. Just so you know."

"I know. Frigid bitch," he shot back.

Crap. I cringed as much as Tiffany did just before she let out a huff opening then slamming the door behind her.

"Vic!" I scolded, turning back to him.

He chuckled. "Truth hurts."

I sighed going back to chopping the veggies. "You've got to stop bringing these women home. It's...gross."

"I know."

My head shot up from my chopping. "Really?"

He pulled a glass from the cabinet and went to the fridge pouring a glass of milk. "Krystal looked good."

Yes! Maybe he was coming to his senses!

"Yeah," I replied as nonchalantly as I could, turning back to the onion and celery and employing major self-control as I tried to keep from jumping up and down and clapping my hands. For some reason, I thought if I showed any enthusiasm it would jinx it all. Weird, I know, but I wasn't about to do anything that might screw things up for them.

"She seeing anyone?"

I was so giddy it was all I could do to remain calm. "No one special," I answered.

"Huh." He finished his milk, setting his glass in the sink then leaned a hip against the counter facing me. "Think she'd be willing to talk?"

I honestly didn't know. But I did know something. "You might give it a week. Or two. I mean, you did just have a...sleepover."

"Yeah," he mumbled. "Hey, I haven't told you but I've been taking a couple online classes."

I looked at him in surprise. "You have?"

"Yeah. If I'm gonna do this bar thing, might as well work toward becoming a manager. Maybe even an owner someday." Pushing off the counter with his hip, he said, "Going to Jeff's for a bit. When will that be ready?" He nodded at the roast.

"Couple hours."

"Be back," he answered pulling on a jacket.

He went out the back door as I threw in the vegetables, arranging them strategically around the meat before seasoning it. Placing the pan in the oven, I realized I wore a huge smile on my face.

CHAPTER 11

I'd given up by the time I went to bed Sunday night.

Drake hadn't texted back and I didn't figure he would.

~*~*~*~*~

Betsy again drove like a dream to class Monday morning which made me think of Drake.

And how I hadn't heard from him.

During class I decided that after work, I'd go by Powers Automotive and apologize to him personally. Not that it'd change things, but it'd make me feel better.

Or worse if he decided he didn't want to talk to me again. Ever.

Just thinking about it made me apprehensive while I drove to Colonial Manor after class as I went through all the scenarios:

1. Drake would smile when he saw me, apologizing for not texting and we'd ride off on a white stallion together. Yeah, yeah. Big fat eye roll.

2. When he saw me, he'd frown then tell me to get the fuck out of there.

3. He'd be making out with that Dina chick and laugh at me, then *they'd* ride off on the stallion together, Dina's giggling trailing behind them.

4. He'd refuse to talk to me altogether, ignoring my presence entirely—as he had the entire week.

5. I'd be cool, he'd be cool, I'd apologize, he'd apologize, then I'd leave never to see him again.

Well, those all sounded fabulous. Ugh.

At work, I clocked in, checked the charts then made a few rounds, checking on the east wing to see if anyone needed new bedding or whatever might've come up during the day. Just before dinner, and an hour before I'd leave, I started setting up the med cups. As soon as I filled them all, I made my rounds, thanking my lucky stars for the millionth time at getting to see the patients this way.

Mrs. Johnson was in an uncommonly good mood, smiling at me when I pushed the cart into her room.

"Holly! You're looking lovely today!" she said.

"Thank you, Aunt Greta. You're looking quite lovely yourself," I told her as I picked up her cup and handed it to her.

"Did Robert take you back? He's a fool if he didn't. Look how beautiful you are today!"

Wow. I wondered if someone's Prozac had accidentally rolled under her door and she'd taken it thinking it was a mint or something.

"Thank you," I answered, waiting for the imminent judgment she always had waiting below the surface to come forth.

But it didn't. She took her meds then smiled, telling me to have a good evening. As I left her room, a surprised smile formed on my face.

Huh. Miracles could actually happen. Shock.

I next wheeled the cart to Mr. Avery's—whoops—Oswald's, room. Friday he'd told me he was going to play basketball against his granddaughter over the weekend, so I couldn't wait to hear how it'd gone.

"Hey, Oswald! How'd the one-on-one game—" I began but pulled up short when I saw that his room was empty, as in all his things were gone.

My hand covered my mouth as my heart began beating rapidly, my breathing speeding up as tears burned the backs of my eyes.

"No," I whispered, telling myself to calm down.

He was staying at his daughter's. Yes, that was it. She'd finally taken time off work so he could live with them for a while. That's what'd happened. He'd told me his granddaughters were so excited about his moving in with them.

I stood in his doorway for a moment longer, convincing myself that, yes, that was what was going on. Then nodding, I wiped a random tear from my cheek that had slipped by and went to finish dispensing meds.

~*~*~*~*~

After work, I sat in Betsy in the nursing home parking lot staring out the windshield as tears streamed down my face.

Susan, the nursing director, had found me outside the last room on my rounds and told me Mr. Avery had passed away over the weekend. She'd apologized all over herself for not getting to me beforehand but she'd been in a meeting. She'd gone on to say that he'd been at his daughter's and had gone peacefully in his sleep, of which I was glad. I'd thanked her for telling me, and after clocking out, I'd hardly been able to hold in my sobs until I got to my truck.

The thought of never seeing Mr. Avery again had my tears coming hard, and I covered my face with my hands as I cried. When someone suddenly knocked at my side window, I jumped then turned to see Drake leaning down looking concernedly at me. I got out of the truck and grabbed him in a hug, my sobs coming anew.

"Shhh," he whispered, rubbing a hand up and down my back.

"I—I didn't...get to...say...goodbye," I said through my tears, the ambiguity of the statement hitting me hard.

"It's okay, baby," he consoled quietly. "He knew you cared about him."

"H-how do you know wh-who I'm t-talking about?" I asked, keeping the side of my head against his chest again sensing the double meaning in our comments.

His hand stilled on my back as he explained, "I went inside to find you. They told me you were upset, so I came out here hoping to catch you."

I buried my face in his soft leather jacket, the feel of his arms around me and the earthy smell of him comforting me more than anything. Crying softly as he held me, my sadness for Mr. Avery and my relief that Drake was there became a dichotomy of confusion in my head.

I pulled back and looked up at him, his face so beautiful in the dim lights of the lot. "Wh-why are you here?"

"Needed to talk to you."

I sniffled and ran my fingers under my eyes waiting to hear what he had to say.

"You going home?"

I nodded.

"Can I follow you back to your place?"

I nodded again watching his eyes roam over my face as if he hadn't seen me in years or maybe he was trying to memorize my features. I didn't know. Then he leaned in slowly, his golden eyes on mine, seeking permission it seemed. When I didn't move away, he touched his lips to mine.

"I'll be right behind you," he promised, opening the truck door for me to get in.

~*~*~*~*~

"I'm sorry for what happened last Tuesday," I apologized, placing a plate with a brownie on it in front of Drake who sat at the table.

We were in my kitchen where I felt most comfortable because if he was going to tell me things wouldn't work out with us, at least I was in a place I liked. But then I semi-panicked thinking I'd hate the kitchen forever if that happened.

Great.

I handed him a bottle of beer—because beer with something sweet always tastes better—then sat across from him, my own brownie and beer in front of me. I was still weepy, of course, but that couldn't be helped. I'd loved Mr. Avery and knew I'd miss him terribly.

"Stop apologizing," Drake said quietly. Then taking a bite from his fork—these were my double chocolate Hershey's syrup brownies that required a fork—he let out a groan. "Fucking amazing, Honor."

"Thanks." I took my own bite and had to agree. They were pretty good.

"What'd you do all week?" he asked a little sheepishly.

I told him about the roast I'd made then my classes, finishing up with yesterday when Tiffany had called me a cunt. "Between her and Jeremiah, I guess March is gonna be Call Honor Any Name but Her Own month," I pointed out with an annoyed shrug.

"C'mere," he said, scooting his chair out a bit from the table.

My brow creased for a moment, then I got up and went to him where he pulled me down to sit sideways in his lap.

"I thought a lot about what happened Tuesday." He pulled the band from my ponytail letting my hair spill down over my shoulders as he ran his hand through it. He tilted his head as he looked at me. "I'm not gonna apologize for how I reacted." When I frowned and turned away, he took my chin in his fingers pulling me back to face him. "But I will tell you I'm sorry how it made you feel." His eyes searched mine and he let my chin go. "Does that make sense?"

"Yes, but if you'd just told me…"

He nodded. "I'll try, Honor. It's just that I protect what's…mine."

I blinked. Then I blinked again. Was he saying I was *his*? I wasn't quite sure how I felt about that. I mean, on the one hand, it was kinda awesome. But on the other, were we even there yet since he was keeping things from me and telling me he had to be careful who he let in his life?

"Oh," was all I could think to say.

He smiled. "Fuckin' cute." His fingers dribbled through my hair as he murmured, "Testing me, babe." Then he shook his head.

"I guess I'm gonna have to learn Drake-speak because half the things you say make no sense to me," I revealed.

At that, he threw his head back and laughed which made me smile. "Like I said, fuckin' cute," he repeated, then sliding a hand under my hair at the back of my head, he pulled me in for a kiss.

And, dear God, what a kiss it was. By the end of it, I was panting and moaning into his mouth, one hand gripping his shoulder so tightly I was probably leaving nail marks, the other clinched hard in the hair at the back of his neck.

"We good?" he pulled back and asked, his eyes full of mirth at the now-sloppy state I was in. Jeez.

I nodded and he gently pushed me to stand as he did the same. He took his plate to the sink where he rinsed it and his fork, finished what was left of his beer and finding the trashcan in the cabinet under the sink, threw it away.

"Walk me out, babe." He held his hand out to me and taking mine led me to the front door where he asked, "Can I see you Wednesday night?"

"Um, yes," I answered.

"How about I bring a pizza and a movie here?"

I twisted my mouth and teased, "You're not gonna bring one of those blow-'em-up-then-chop-'em-to-pieces-guy movies, are you?"

He chuckled. "Well, I *am* a guy."

"How about I pick the movie? I promise it'll be something we'll both like," I assured.

"Horror?"

"Comedy."

He raised an eyebrow and warned, "Just want you to know, I judge people by their taste in movies. This could make or break us." Well, crap. Now I was a little nervous. He went on to explain, "Zane pulled up *Zombeavers* on Netflix last year saying it was hilarious and I haven't spoken to him since."

Nervousness gone, I started giggling and couldn't stop.

"It's really not that funny, Honor," he stated all serious, which made me laugh even harder. "Worst hour of my fuckin' life."

Oh, God. I was crying.

"Laugh all you want, baby. Won't be funny when I'm giving *you* the silent treatment," he said with a grin so I knew he was playing. He wrapped his arms around my waist smiling down at me. "Doubt I could stay mad at you for long, though."

I wanted to say that he had for a week, but stopped myself. Instead I said, "I want to thank you."

"For?"

"For making my bad day better."

"Ditto." He leaned down and brushed his lips against mine, whispered a goodnight, and after ordering me to lock the door, at which I rolled my eyes, he was gone.

CHAPTER 12

"Your father was my favorite." My voice caught for a moment. "A-and I loved him like he was my own," I told Mr. Avery's daughter after the funeral.

"You must be Honor," she replied with a sad smile. "He talked so highly of you."

"I'll miss him so much," I said with a sniff.

"Thank you for taking such good care of him," she said, wiping a tear away as I did the same.

"Of course."

"Oh, he wanted you to have this." She pulled something from the pocket of her dress then looking down at it, gave a bewildered smile before handing it to me.

Gazing at what she'd given me, I saw it was the knight from his chess set and I choked out a sob.

"I'm not sure what it means," she said. "He just said you'd get it."

"I do," I answered with a nod. "Thank you."

I left the church and drove home, and in my bedroom, placed the knight on my dresser where I knew I'd always see it.

~*~*~*~*~

"Not bad," Drake said Wednesday night when the credits of the movie rolled.

He'd called the night before to make sure I was okay, knowing I'd gone to Mr. Avery's funeral, and we'd ended up talking for several hours. I'd told him about the knight, which he thought was awesome, and I'd learned that he was the oldest of his five brothers—yeesh, his poor mom.

I'd found out that Kase was twenty-four and a computer security analyst at a local well-known computer company; Zane was twenty-three and had just gotten a job as a police officer; Blaze was twenty-one, like me, and finishing up his degree in finance along with playing football; Wilder, at twenty-one was lead singer and guitarist in a band; and Titus had just turned nineteen and was taking classes in auto-body at a technical school, planning to work as a mechanic for Drake someday but eventually helping him add a body shop to the garage.

Good grief. So many to keep up with!

"I'm gonna need to write all this down," I'd replied with a chuckle.

Now we sat on the couch after watching the movie I'd picked. I glanced at him, looking so hot in his blue, plaid button up that was half tucked in over a black t-shirt.

We'd watched *Nothing to Lose*, an older movie which I'd always thought was hysterical and starred Martin Lawrence.

Drawing my legs up and putting my bare feet on the couch, I wrapped my arms around my legs and rested the side of my head on my knees looking at him. "You liked it?"

He nodded. "Best part?" he said. When I raised my eyebrows, he continued. "Well, other than the spider scene, you sittin' here on the couch next to me."

I smiled. "I think under all your badass exterior, you're really a softy at heart," I teased which got me narrowed eyes and made me giggle.

I felt really good about where we were right then in the relationship, having weathered a small storm and come out stronger. We'd talked a lot over pizza, with Drake sharing a lot more about himself and his family and also telling me more of what he wanted for his future. I was getting to know him a lot better and I liked everything I was learning about him.

After my comment, he turned fast, tackling me to where I now lay with my back to the sofa with him on top.

"Nothing soft about me, babe," he rumbled before his lips suddenly crashed down on mine.

And I was ready. I'd waited long enough. God, I wanted him so badly.

I moaned into his mouth, my hips involuntarily rising to meet his, amping up everything which was awesome. His hands were now everywhere, one under my shirt, grasping my breast over my bra where he rolled my nipple between his thumb and finger making me cry out. His other hand slid down between us, over my belly and into my jeans, down inside my panties where he glided his fingers through my folds.

"Oh, God, yes," I breathed as he paid particular attention to my clitoris, his fingers on either side, moving with purpose, extracting whimpers and mewls and other incoherent sounds to issue from my mouth.

When he dipped a finger inside, curling it and pressing it into me, gliding it over that secret spot, I threw my head back, arching up off the couch, my mouth open as I breathed out an *Oh fuck!* as I came hard, every muscle tensing, shaking, as white hot bolts of energy slammed through me.

Holy hell. He'd barely touched me and I'd orgasmed. Just. Like. That.

Shit!

"Jesus," I heard him murmur from above me.

Opening my eyes and breathing hard, I looked up at him in awe, just as surprised as he was at my response to his touch.

Damn, the man was good.

"Make love to me, Drake," I uttered between breaths.

Then I watched as he sucked in a breath and went still.

Crap!

He hesitated!

God, had I read him wrong? He'd made it clear a couple times—or so I'd thought—that he wanted me, but now I guessed I was mistaken.

Our eyes held for a moment, his full of indecision—why was he so guarded?—and I started to sit up.

"It's okay. We don't—" I began when he suddenly scooped me up bridal style standing and carrying me down the hall quickly. I guess he did want me after all?

Well, all right then.

"Room?" he bit out.

"Last to the right," I answered, almost dizzy from being moved so fast. Dang.

He burst into my bedroom and in the light from the hall, saw my bed and threw me on it where I let out a yelp as I bounced a couple times. Dang.

"Light," he ordered and I reached over to turn on my bedside lamp.

He went back to the door then stood there looking at me, hand stroking his chin and still freaking hesitating, as if assessing the situation, like he was really thinking it over...afraid he was making a mistake.

Okay. That was it. I wasn't begging someone to have sex with me for God's sake.

And a big fat P.S. here—This all made me feel like shit.

I put my feet to the floor and stood. "Drake, I'm not gonna force—"

"Quiet," he interrupted making me look at him. Eyes boring into mine, he commanded, "Ass back on the bed."

Was he serious?

I narrowed my eyes at him and seeing how he didn't budge, figured he was.

Damn it.

I crawled back onto the bed, then sitting with my knees up, elbows resting on them, I restated, "We don't have to do—"

"I said quiet."

I shook my head. "God. You're so boss—"

His eyes burned into mine making me stop talking as he closed and locked my door then he ground out, "You ever fuckin' listen?"

Oookay.

My legs straightened as I got ready to get off my bed again. "Well, this has been romantic and all..." I shared then stopped talking when he stalked toward me removing his shirt then reaching behind his head and pulling his t-shirt off.

And, holy mother of frick. His body was magnificent: abs that had ripples upon ripples, pecs that were solid as steel, and biceps that bulged as he unbuckled his belt and unbuttoned his jeans.

And the tattoos. Holy cow.

My eyes got big as I stared at his chest that had swirls of colors surrounding something at the center...an angel of death? Then I noticed tribal-type art on his left shoulder I'd seen at the flag football game and saw the name "Will" in it. Which reminded me he'd never answered when I'd asked about him. So I tried again. "Who's Will?"

"Take off your shirt," he instructed darkly, standing at the foot of my bed and looking down at me like he wanted to devour me, so sexy standing there shirtless, jeans undone.

I was so confused as to what to do, my emotions all over the place at that point. He wouldn't answer me about Will, he acted as if he had to convince himself to have sex with me, and now he was being super bossy again.

"Take it off, Honor," he stated, his voice authoritative as always.

I admit I was kind of scared, yet aroused, thrilled, at his domineering demeanor as I began unbuttoning my shirt then removed it.

"Jeans."

I looked at him waiting for him to crack but that wasn't going to happen I now saw, his face deadly serious, eyes glittering as he watched me.

I unzipped my jeans and lying back, pulled them off, tossing them to the bedside floor near my shirt. When I sat back up, I gazed at him then sucked in a breath feeling my womb dip at the way he was staring at my panties, his tongue coming out as he licked his lips before biting his bottom one.

God.

His eyes took their time making their way to mine as they drifted up my body.

"Good girl," he praised.

Sweet Jesus, this was hot. I was literally panting now, my panties soaked with my need. And it felt like I was going to come again just from his slow and deliberate seduction with only his friggin' eyes. Gah!

He sat on the edge of the bed, seeming to take his time as he unlaced his boots then took them off before standing again. Then I saw him jerk his chin up slightly and knew he wanted me to continue getting naked.

I was so in sync with him just then and found I was beginning to understand his ways. Eyes staying on his, I saw his crinkle just a bit at the sides showing he was pleased that I was doing what he'd wordlessly asked when I reached a hand behind and unhooked my bra letting it slide slowly down my arms before removing it. Next, my thumbs went inside the waistband of my panties and raising up slightly for a second, I pulled them down my legs and off.

"Lean back and spread your legs for me."

This was so intense, so different from any experience I'd had, and I found I was a bit reluctant. The sides of his eyes creased again then he gave me a barely discernible nod, and breathing out, I did as I was told, going back on my elbows and letting my legs fall apart.

"Touch yourself."

Oh, God.

God!

My heart was about to pound out of my chest as I bit the inside of my lip in uncertainty. But I'd trusted him this far, so swallowing roughly I moved my hand down knowing I'd come the minute I made contact which I did. Shit! My back arched up off the bed and my head fell back as I screamed out, "Oh, fuck!"

Immediately, my legs were over his shoulders then his mouth was between my legs where he sucked and licked, his tongue entering me, fucking me, keeping my orgasm going.

Oh my.

"Want you to coat my chin, baby," he growled as he sucked hard on my clitoris.

"Drake!" I cried as my body shuddered with more spasms, my legs trembling on his shoulders as he tasted every bit of me.

Lowering me gently to the bed, he stood tall and eyes on mine, used his finger to wipe his chin before putting it between his lips to suck my juices off it.

Damn.

Breathing hard, I watched as he put a knee to the bed and crawled up to hover over me. Then looking down at me, he uttered, "We do this, you're not pulling any shit again like you did the other night."

It took a second for my cloudy brain to catch up and grasp what he'd said.

Wait. What?

"Uh," was all my climax-fogged brain could get out.

"Fuck," he drawled out staring down at my body. "Fucking beautiful just like I knew you would be."

I found my voice and whispered, "What do you mean by 'shit like I did the other night'?" because I thought it was pretty important that he clarify.

His eyes came up to mine and he explained. "If I sense you're in danger, I need you to listen."

"Oh," I mumbled. "Well, okay."

His eyes twinkled and he kissed me roughly. Then he was gone, standing at the side of the bed reaching into his back pocket and pulling out his wallet to retrieve a condom. As he slid his jeans and boxer briefs down, I saw his hard cock spring out and stand brilliantly at attention, and oh my word, it matched the rest of his glorious body and it really *was* a masterpiece.

Dear God, all of him was beautiful.

He put on the condom then covered my body once again with his, resting on his elbows as I cradled his hips between my legs. Looking down at me, eyes piercing mine, he stated, "This is important to me, Honor. I don't fuck around like most guys. Got too much on the line to do that shit."

Even as I was trying to decipher what he meant by his having a lot on the line, when I felt the head of his cock at my opening, my heightened libido took over as my hips surged toward him, wanting him inside.

"So you get me, yeah?"

Damn it. I wasn't completely sure what he was saying or what I was getting myself into. I had so many questions. But I didn't listen to my brain because my body needed him, craved him at that moment, so instead, I breathed, "Yeah."

"Good," he said low, his eyes sparkling with what looked like relief, like he'd heard what he needed to hear. He slid his hand behind my knee and stretched my leg all the way up as I watched. "Eyes," he ordered and just as I brought my eyes up to his, he drove in deep.

"Oh, God!" I cried out at his hard thrust inside, feeling as if he was touching my very soul.

"Ah, fuck," he rasped as his hips started moving, burying himself so deep with each push forward, I gasped every time. "So fucking tight, Honor. Jesus fuck!"

My fingernails scored into his back but I couldn't help it. He was big. Huge. If I hadn't been primed, he'd have ripped me in two. But the way he was moving now, the delicious friction he created as his hips pistoned into mine, another climax was building and, oh my God, this was pure heaven.

Leaning down, he covered my mouth with his, swallowing my moans just as I peaked again.

"That's it, baby. Fucking milk my cock with that sweet pussy," he groaned against my lips.

God.

The way he talked had my head reeling, turning me on like no one else had ever done before.

He dropped my leg and slid his hands under my bottom, pulling my hips up as he began slamming inside powerfully, going so deep, oh, God, so deep, that I cried out again.

Sweet Jesus.

"Like me fucking you, don't you, baby?" he said huskily.

"Yes," I moaned.

"Mm, let's see if you like this," he growled, pulling out and flipping me to my belly, then pulling my hips up, drove inside, going so deep and thrusting so hard, I had to grab the blanket to stay in place.

Snaking a hand around he splayed it across my belly as his other hand moved up to twist in my hair pulling me up so my back was now against his front.

As he pumped his hips, his mouth was at my ear and he ground out, "More than I fucking dreamed it'd be." His hand at my stomach slid down to move in circles on me at the same time his other let go of my hair and curled around to the front where he gripped me by my chin.

"I-I can't come again," I whimpered, my body worn out.

"You can. Gonna come, babe. Want you with me."

I exploded just as I heard him grunt, and he buried himself to the hilt inside me as I collapsed back limply against his hard body.

Mother fricking frick.

So this was what all the hubbub was about.

The sex I'd had with the two guys I'd been with before was nothing compared to this.

Wow.

Drake moved us forward to lie down then lips brushing my shoulder, he slowly pulled out.

"Be back," he said, kissing the side of my head.

I had no idea when or if he made it back because I passed out seconds later.

CHAPTER 13

I awoke to an empty bed and frowned.

I stretched huge, sore in all the good places and had to smile thinking about the night before with Drake. Then turning to the side, I grabbed my cell off the nightstand—how it got there, I had no idea because I'd left it on the coffee table in the living room—and read the text that was waiting for me.

Text Message—Thurs, Mar 10, 4:39 a.m.

Drake: Miss you already, babe. Heard Victor come in, talked with him a sec then left. Call you later

I smiled again as I texted back.

Text Message—Thurs, Mar 10, 7:09 a.m.

Me: I miss you too. Was Vic shocked to see you? And thanks for bringing my phone in here

Text Message—Thurs, Mar 10, 7:12 a.m.

Drake: He was more scared. Screamed like a little girl. Welcome

I giggled. Oh, that was priceless. I'd have to tease Vic about it later.

Me: That's awesome lol Wanna come to dinner tonight?

Drake: Can't. Webinar for class tonight, plans for the weekend. Can I see you Monday?

Well, damn. Of course, my chick-brain immediately went to a bad place thinking he had a date over the weekend. And for all I knew, that could very well be what was going on.

Text Message—Thurs, Mar 10, 7:16 a.m.

Me: I'll check and let you know later

There. Two could play this game.

Drake: Okay. You were amazing last night

I felt my face get red wondering what I should say back.

Me: You were too...

Drake: Call you later x

Me: Okay. Bye xo

Before I let my head go into overthinking territory, I decided to drop it. He said he missed me, so that counted for something, right? Besides, we weren't exclusive. He could be dating thirty other women for all I knew.

And on that depressing thought, I got up to get ready for class.

~*~*~*~*~

That night after getting home from work, my phone rang.

"Hey, babe. Can't talk long. I've got a shit ton of homework. Just wanted to say hi," Drake said when I answered.

"Hi! I understand. Go get 'em, tiger," I replied with a chuckle.

"Fuckin' cute, Honor. I wasn't busy, I'd come over and spank your gorgeous ass."

My eyes went wide. He'd spank me? I had no idea how to feel about that.

"Um, okay." Brilliant response, I know.

He chuckled sexily. "See you haven't been spanked before, huh?"

"Not since I was little when I accidentally threw out Mom's chicken broth for dinner she had on the stove thinking it was dirty water."

"You shouldn't have been spanked for an accident."

"Yeah, well, tell my mom that."

"I have a feeling you'd like my spankings, though," he said darkly, intriguingly.

"Uh..."

"Fuck. I've gotta go before you make me wanna come over and prove it. Talk to you tomorrow?"

"Yes, sure."

"Later, babe."

After ending the call, I immediately called Krystal.

"What's up?" she answered.

"Okay, I'm trying not to wig out here, but Drake just said he'd spank me."

She laughed. "I take it you've never been spanked sexually before."

"Why's everyone so concerned about my sex life suddenly? First Drake now you. I'm starting to feel inadequate here!"

"Nah. It's just one of those things you need to try. You either like it or you don't," she assured.

"You've been spanked?" I asked, kind of in shock.

She giggled. "Victor liked...exploring lots of things."

"Oh, yuck." I heard her giggling harder. "Gross. Now every time I look at you two I'm gonna gag."

I wanted to tell her that Vic might be calling her but held back just in case he didn't follow through. Although there'd been no heel clicking this morning when I got ready for school, which was a good start, I never knew what he was going to do.

"Oh, I can tell you lots of sordid things we did," she replied with a snort.

"Going now. Talk to you later. Bye," I said and hung up, shuddering because I didn't ever want to hear about anything she and Vic had done. I also realized she'd probably been right to keep their breakup details mum because I'd basically just shown I couldn't be objective.

Jeez.

~*~*~*~*~

The next night, Drake texted close to midnight after I'd already gone to sleep so I didn't get it until Saturday morning. He'd just texted to say hi so I texted back the same but got no reply.

He didn't text back until after I was asleep again, so I got his text Sunday morning, I texted back, and, again, got no answer.

And I loved that my imagination was going wild telling me he was dating fifty supermodels and I needed to move on. Gotta love the human brain. All I could do was throw it a big middle finger, reminding myself I'd be fine with or without him even though I knew the latter would hurt like a son-of-a-bitch.

Just as I was drifting off Sunday night, my phone rang.

"Babe," Drake replied when I answered. "Can't do tomorrow night. My parents and aunt and uncle are going out of town for two weeks and I've got the shop. No evenings free until they get back. You wanna swing by and say hi Friday, that'd be good."

I frowned. He didn't want to see me until Friday? Hm. "I can do that. Can I ask where they're going?" I said.

"Of course, you can."

There we went again.

"Where are they going?" I asked, not bothering to keep the annoyance out of my voice.

He chuckled. "Funeral in New Jersey. My great-uncle passed away, and they haven't gotten to see the family in years, so they thought they'd make use of the time while there and visit."

"Oh. I'm sorry about your uncle," I answered.

"Thanks. I didn't really know him. Think I saw him once but I was little so I don't really remember."

"That's too bad."

"Yeah. Well, whaddya gonna do. Anyway, I wanna see you, just can't take time to get away."

"Okay," I replied. "Well, since I live farther away and you're closer to the shop, maybe I could come over to your place one of these nights?"

"Not a good idea," he answered abruptly which pinged my senses and threw up all kinds of red flags.

My thoughts instantly went to, he's married and doesn't want me to know, or he's into something illegal and running it out of his house and doesn't want me to see it.

"Oh."

"Just come by the garage Friday after you get off work."

"I'll try."

"Do it," he ordered.

God.

"Okay."

We hung up and I lay awake wondering what he was hiding and if I really wanted to stay involved with him.

It was after two by the time I fell asleep.

~*~*~*~*~

After work Friday, I wasn't sure what to do.

I wanted to see Drake, but things just seemed kind of strained. We'd texted on and off during the week, he'd called Wednesday night and we'd talked for an hour but not about anything major. He was still closed off, and I felt sure he was hiding something.

Or had I just made shit up in my own head?

I mean, we'd gone from having mind-blowing sex to not seeing each other for over a week. What was going on? Was he juggling me along with a few other women? He'd told me he didn't sleep around, but maybe his definition of that was different from mine. And he'd said he had a lot on his plate, but was that plate filled with gorgeous chicks?

God. Sometimes I hated being a woman with all the emotions that just drove me crazy.

I made my decision as I left Colonial Manor's parking lot, turning and heading to the garage.

It was a quarter to six when I pulled up seeing there were no cars sitting outside. Going into the service area, it was like the first time I'd been there—empty. I looked through the window on the door into the garage and saw Drake looking under a car hood, so opening the door I went in.

"Hey," I called walking to where he was working, nervously playing with the zipper on my jacket. He stood straight and I watched as his lips curled into a smirk. "Whatcha doin—"

He grabbed me in his arms and planted a big one on me, his tongue finding mine to tangle with it. His hand dropped down and grabbed my butt as he jerked me against him hard. When he pulled back, he looked at me as if I were the only ice cube in the Sahara Desert.

"Fucking missed you, baby." He touched his lips to mine then said, "Be right back."

He left the garage and went into the service area then came back a minute later, his eyes hot on mine.

"So what've you been up—"

I didn't get to finish my question because his mouth slammed down on mine in a bruising kiss then he picked me up to where I had to wrap my legs around his waist. Sitting me on a car hood, he pulled away and gazed at me.

"Fucking missed you..." he repeated. "Need to be inside you, Honor. Can you handle it?"

God, yes, I could handle it. His kisses had made my body instantly react to him, and I was pretty sure I was more than ready.

"Yes," I replied breathily.

He had one of my scrubs pantlegs down and off then was unbuttoning his jeans and putting a condom on before I knew it. Moving forward, he pulled me to the edge of the hood where I wrapped my legs around his hips then he was inside.

"Oh, my God," I whispered at how fully he filled me.

He captured my mouth with his again, then thrusting his hips hard, pounding them mercilessly against me, he fucked me like he had the first time. It was rough, it was hard, and I loved it.

"You feel so goddamned good," he groaned against my lips, his hand moving up, wrapping into my ponytail and jerking my head back. He then attacked my neck with kisses, with soft licks and hard sucks, punishing horse bites and I came. "Fuck," he growled as I pulsed around him.

His mouth landed and stayed on mine as he continued to pound into me before burying himself deep with a groan. Remaining inside, he resumed kissing me but this kiss was different. It was soft and sweet and left me feeling high when he pulled away.

"Missed my girl," he muttered putting his forehead to mine.

"I missed you too," I admitted. And, I was his girl? All the stupid negative thoughts I'd had about him melted away as he kissed me gently again. So this was the sweet he'd talked about. I liked it.

"Stay here," he said, pulling out of me. He went to a trash can and removed the condom, throwing it away then tucked himself back into his jeans. Coming back, he helped me down from the car holding my hips to keep me steady on my wobbly orgasm legs as I pulled my pants leg back on.

"Thanks," I whispered.

"Thank you for showing up. So fucking glad you did." He kissed me again before taking my hand and leading me back into the service area. "You hungry?" he asked.

"Kinda."

He led me to a small table in the corner and pulled out the chair having me sit. Then he went to a counter and grabbed a bag.

"Had these delivered from Earl's earlier hoping you'd come." He waggled his eyebrows at his bad pun and I snorted.

This was the side of him I liked. The easygoing, open side, not the one that was so cautious.

He pulled out two wrapped sandwiches setting one in front of me. "Hope you like brisket?" At my nod, he next laid out two bags of chips then going to the small fridge in the corner brought back two bottles of root beer.

"Thank you. I love their sandwiches," I declared, taking a bite.

"You been doing okay?" he asked, mouth full. "Heard from Jeremiah?"

I nodded my head and after swallowing, told him, "He's called a couple times but I haven't called back."

His face got serious. "Next time, you take his call and find out what he wants. Then you let me know if you have any problems."

"I don't foresee any but I'll let you know."

As I ate, I built the courage to ask him the questions that'd been occupying the better part of my head for a while. I was afraid he'd get mad saying it was none of my business, but then again, he'd just had his dick inside me, so, yeah, I felt maybe it was my business.

"Can I ask you something?"

He chewed as he looked at me. "Sure."

I set my sandwich down and licked my lips. "I was wondering where you were last weekend and also why I can't come to your house?"

There. Two birds, one stone and all.

I picked my sandwich back up and took a bite waiting for him to answer.

He cleared his throat then took a drink. "Last weekend was...personal."

"Are you dating other women?" His narrowed eyes had me hurrying to say, "Because that's fine but I'm looking for more so..." I trailed off when his eyes went hard.

"Told you I don't fuck around, Honor."

"Well, who's Will?" I blurted.

He blew out a breath just as his phone rang. Glancing at the screen, he apologized saying it was his dad and he needed to take it.

Getting up from the table and going behind the counter, I heard him talking about a part that was supposed to have shipped as he clicked on the keyboard.

"I'll call them as soon as I get off here. Okay. Yeah. I'll let you know," he said before hanging up.

I'd finished eating and stood to throw my wrappers away.

"Gotta make another call," he said, still typing on the computer.

"I need to go anyway," I said.

He looked up at me and something flashed in his eyes. Anger? Hurt? "Look. We've known each other, what, about a month," he stated.

"I know. It's none of my business."

He ran a hand over his face. "It can be your business, Honor. I just have to be sure."

"Meaning?" I pried.

"Meaning I have to be fucking sure." We had a stare-off and he looked away first. "Sorry. I need to make this call before they close."

"'Bye, Drake," I said walking toward the door.

"I'll call you later," he promised just before the door closed behind me.

~*~*~*~*~

"I think I'm permanently PMSing," I told Krystal.

I'd gone by her place after leaving Drake's on the off chance that she'd be there. I'd just caught her as she was leaving for her parents'.

"You've had a lot going on, honey. Mr. Avery passing, school, work, Drake, Jeremiah. But you're strong and will be fine," she claimed.

"I do have a lot." I sighed. I then told her what Drake had said when I'd asked my questions.

"Well, you really haven't known each other for very long," she declared. "I think he wants to tell you, but like he said, he has to be sure."

"Yeah, but his secrets must be something big since he's been pretty open about everything else."

"They must be," she stated.

I looked at her and shrugged. "I think I just need to relax, you know? Just enjoy what we have. When he's ready, he'll tell me."

"Thatta girl," she replied with a snicker.

"What?"

"You just said everything to yourself that I would've said to you." She nodded. "But I'm sure he'll open up the longer you're together," she assured.

"I just wanna know stuff," I whined. Then it hit me. "Maybe I'm too nosy."

She laughed. "Nah. I think you've just had so many crap people in your life you want everything up front, that's all. Trust him, On. He'll open up soon, I bet."

"I hope so. It just makes me feel bad that he thinks he can't tell me stuff." I looked at her. "I mean, I'm thinking Will might be his son or maybe his grandpa he's taking care of...or his gay lover." She snorted. "I'm rushing things with him, aren't I?"

"Yep."

"I just don't wanna be blindsided, you know? I hate that shit."

She nodded then said, "Hey, that new Greek restaurant opened up last weekend. Wanna go tomorrow night? I heard their pastitsio is amazing!"

"Sure. Sounds good," I replied. I looked at her for a moment, feeling bad for complaining about Drake having secrets when I had one of my own. "I need to tell you something."

She raised her eyebrows as she waited.

Proceeding with caution, I revealed, "It's about Vic." I wasn't sure how she'd take his asking about her, and I got ready for her to tell me to stop, that she didn't want to know anything about him.

"Don't tell me he's met someone!"

I jerked my head back surprised by her statement. "God, no!" Totally not the response from her that I expected. I knew her well enough to know she'd fight this. That she'd blow it off, but I was now pleasantly surprised. Maybe there was hope of their reuniting after all.

"Good." She looked relieved. "Okay, what is it?"

"Wait a minute. You're okay with him sleeping around but you'd be upset if he met someone he liked?"

"I'm not *okay* with it, but as long as that's what he's doing, I know he's not gonna fall for anyone."

"You still love him," I whispered. Holy crap!

"I don't know. I mean, no!" she stated, her face twisting into a frown, which made me sad because she so totally still loved him.

"He, uh, asked about you."

She then looked at me in confusion. "He did?"

"Yeah, after he saw you the other day. He wanted to know if you'd talk to him." I saw her brow go up. "He hasn't been bringing anyone home either," I rushed to say.

"Really," she murmured skeptically, tossing her hair behind her shoulder in annoyance. Ah. *There* was the reaction I'd expected to get.

"He hasn't. And he's been taking online classes so he can get his business degree to become a manager at the bar, maybe even an owner someday, he said."

"Well, look at him go. Maybe he's finally growing up," she answered flippantly as if she couldn't have cared less. And I saw she'd shut down.

"Maybe." I let it go because I'd only wanted to plant the idea of talking to him in her head, not argue with her about it. "Okay, well, I'll let you get to your parents' house. Tell them I said hi. Text me later."

Even though she tried acting as if that last bit of our conversation about Vic hadn't happened, I could see the thoughts racing in her head. I wanted to squeal in glee, but I kept my cool because that would just piss her off.

We walked out together and said our goodbyes then drove off in different directions.

CHAPTER 14

Walking into my house, I felt that something was off.

I'd used the back door coming into the kitchen, and upon entering after turning on the light, I was suddenly paralyzed with fear thinking I heard someone moving around inside the house. Before I could leave from the way I'd come, Jeremiah walked around the corner looking just as shocked at seeing me as I know I did when I saw him.

"What the fuck are you doing here?" I hissed, scared shitless.

"Came to get my stuff," he said now all casual. I noticed he had a hoodie and a couple shirts over his arm.

"So you just broke in?" I yelled.

"If you'd take my fucking calls, I wouldn't have had to!"

"I'm calling the police!" I said, reaching inside my purse for my phone.

"Don't, Honor. I'm leaving. I just wanted to get my things."

I held my phone ready to dial 911 watching as he walked farther into the kitchen coming right toward me. I hate to admit it, but I flinched when he grabbed a brownie off the plate on the counter next to me and took a bite.

"Think I'll miss your cooking the most," he said, mouth full and shaking the brownie at me as he spoke. I could tell he was pleased he'd scared me as he gave me a smirk before leaving.

Holy shit.

My heart was in my throat as I rushed to the back door locking it then I called Victor.

"Yeah? I don't have a lot of time," he answered.

"Jeremiah broke into the house!"

"What?"

"I just got home and he was in here getting some things of his I had!" I slid down the door landing with my butt on the floor and started crying. God. That had been some scary shit.

"That little fucker!"

I sniffed. "N-no. It's my fault. I haven't been taking his calls and I should have."

"Doesn't give him the right to break the fuck in!"

"I-I don't even know h-how he got inside," I stammered. "Sh-should I call the police?"

"No. I'll get someone to cover. I'm coming home to check around. Go to Krystal's."

"Do we need to get an alarm?" I questioned as I stood, looking around to see if anything was missing. God.

I heard him talking to someone then he came back on the line. "I'll look into an alarm. I'm on my way out the door. Go to Krystal's. Now."

"Okay. Be careful. You sure you don't want me to call the police?"

I could tell he was jogging to his bike when he yelled, "No! Get your ass out of there! Now!"

"Going now. I love you. See you in the morning."

We hung up and I made my way outside, locking the door behind me. And now I was afraid Jeremiah had stuck around and was going to attack me. Gah! On high alert, I ran to Betsy, got in, started her and took off.

I next called Krystal. "Jeremiah broke into my house!"

"What!"

I told her what'd happened asking if I could come back over.

"Of course! I'm on my way back from Mom and Dad's anyway. I'll meet you there. Oh, my God, that's so scary!"

"I know." I was definitely rattled.

When I got to her place, she'd apparently just pulled in too, meeting me at Betsy's door as I got out and giving me a hug.

"That bastard!" she fumed as we walked inside her apartment. She immediately went to the fridge, got out a bottle of wine and poured us each a full glass.

"Let me get my coat off first," I said with an uneasy chuckle.

"Psh. Fuck that, On." She held out a glass as I was taking off my jacket. "You need something to relax you in your veins right about now."

I hung my coat on the rack then taking the wine, downed it because she was right.

"Thatta girl," she said, reaching for my glass and refilling it. "Here."

I drank down that one too.

"Whoa, easy there, woman," Krystal said giving me another full glass.

This one I sipped—kind of—knowing that since I wasn't a big drinker, the first two glasses would start *taking* effect soon, meaning I'd get giggly, chatty, act like an idiot, then I'd finally get tired and pass out. Yippee.

She hung her jacket up as I sat on the couch then coming over, she sat too saying, "So you walked in and he was there?"

I told her I'd sensed something was off, and that I'd about had a heart attack when Jeremiah had walked into the kitchen. Then I explained how he'd approached me and taken a brownie.

"What an asshole. How'd he get in?"

"I have no idea. Vic's there checking things out now," I said. "But it's still kinda my fault. I should've answered his calls." She gave me a look that made me giggle. Thanks, wine. "What?" I asked.

"Do you hear yourself right now? No decent person would break into someone's house. He could've left a voicemail or, hell, texted you, letting you know he wanted to meet you to pick his shit up! You're not at fault at all."

She did have a point. "You're right. I mean, what if I'd pulled out my nine and busted a cap in his ass?" I put my hand over my mouth melodramatically. "I could've killed him!" I burst out laughing.

"Yeah. Because you so have a gun. Okay, lightweight. Enough wine for you," she said with a snort getting up and taking my glass from me as she went to the kitchen.

My phone rang. "That's probably Vic." I grabbed my cell out of my purse and answered it. "Hey. Did you find out how the fucker got in?"

"What're you talking about?" Drake asked.

"Oh, hey, *Drake*," I replied, bugging my eyes at Krystal as she came back into the living room. "I need to tell you I'm sorry," I blurted.

I heard his low chuckle. "About?"

"Well, you might not have noticed, but I've been a jerk to you," I admitted.

"Nah," he drawled. "You're good."

"I just wish we were at the point where you trusted me to tell me some things."

"We're getting there, babe. Give it time."

"Okay. I just can't help being a little antsy-pantsed sometimes," I informed him.

"As long as you stay sweet, we're good. So what did you mean when you answered?" he asked.

"Oh! Well, after I left the garage, I went to Krystal's. She was getting ready to go to her parents but she stayed and talked to me. Isn't she the sweetest? And her parents! I love them so much! They treat me like I'm their daughter too! How cool is that?" I looked at Krystal and nodded because all I'd said was true.

"Honor?" Drake called.

"Yeah?"

"What did you mean when you answered?"

"Huh?"

"You asked how the fucker got in. What did you mean?" he asked again.

"Oh! Jeremiah broke into my house! I got home and it felt weird, and then he just strolled right into the kitchen like no big freaking deal! He even ate a brownie! Can you believe that? He's such a jerk!"

"He broke into your house? Fuck!"

"Yep. I don't know how, though. Vic's there trying to find out. And you know what else? I think he took one of Vic's hoodies!"

"You've been drinking," he deduced.

I giggled. "Yep. Krys gave me some wine to help my nerves and I kinda chugged it. I don't drink a lot so when I do, whew! I get toasted!" I giggled some more.

"Babe, give the phone to Krystal," he said.

I frowned. "You don't like talking to me?"

"I do but I need to talk to her."

"Why?"

"Baby, just give her the phone," he ordered.

"I love it when you call me that," I said dreamily letting out a sigh. Then my eyes opened and I added, my tone now serious, "But you know what I don't like? Bossiness." I nodded. "And speaking of bossiness, Vic was bossy to me tonight. He told me to get my ass out of the house. How rude is that?"

"Honor..."

"But you know when I do like bossiness?" I said low into the phone. "I liked it when you bossed me in the bedroom. That was hot." I giggled even more.

"Honor..."

"Oh, my gosh. I'm kinda drunk, huh?"

He chuckled. "I guess you are. Do me a favor and let me talk to Krystal for a second, okay?"

I rolled my eyes. "Oh, all right." I held my phone out to her. "Here!"

"Hello?" she asked.

"It's Drake," I whispered loudly.

She nodded and held a finger to her mouth telling me to be quiet.

"Am I being loud?" I asked with a yawn.

She nodded again as she listened. Then I heard her give him Vic's phone number and I wondered what was going on.

So I asked, "What's going on?" probably loudly because Krystal put her finger to her mouth again.

While she had my phone, I was suddenly tired and lay down on my side on the couch, pulling the afghan off the back of it to cover myself and curling my legs up. "Okay, hang on," I heard her say.

I heard her call my name and felt a nudge on my shoulder. Opening my eyes, I saw her holding the phone out to me which I took. "Hullo?" I answered sleepily.

"Babe, I'm gonna call your brother to see what he found out, okay?"

"You know what?"

"What?"

"You and Vic are a lot alike. You're bossy, he's bossy. You can sometimes be—and I'm sorry to say this but it's the truth—a real jerk and so can he." I yawned.

"I know, baby. I'm gonna hang up and call him. You should go lie down."

"I'm already lying down, Mr. Bossypants." I yawned again. "But I'm really not that tired."

"I know you're not, just try it. I'll talk to you later, okay?"

"'Kay. Bye, Drake," I said and was out.

~*~*~*~*~

"Ow," I moaned holding my head as I sat up on the couch the next morning. "How can I have a hangover from only two glasses of wine?"

"Morning, Megara," she said with a sweet smile.

"Hey, Aurora," I answered, squinting my eyes because her living room was too freaking bright.

When we were in fifth grade, we'd decided we were really Disney princesses, and with her blond hair and sweet and cheery disposition, Krystal was a shoe-in for Sleeping Beauty. My auburn hair along with my snarkiness had tied me to the cynical Megara, who technically wasn't a princess, but we'd made her one anyway.

"Three," Krystal stated.

"Huh?" I questioned, scrunching up my face.

She chuckled from where she sat in the recliner, legs over the arm and watching that same crappy reality show while she ate one of the brownies I'd made for her. "You had three glasses. And it was a marsala. Higher alcohol content. But there's water and aspirin on the end table for you." She nodded toward it.

I narrowed my eyes at her as I reached for the glass of water and pills. "And you didn't think to tell me it was more..." I looked for the word since my brain refused to work. "Alcohol-y?"

She shrugged. "Mom brought it back from Sicily last year and I was waiting for a good time to use it." She picked up a glass of milk from the table and took a drink.

"And Jeremiah breaking in was a good time?" I rubbed my hands over my face.

"As good as any. You hungry?" She held out a brownie.

"No. Gross. I feel like shit."

She pulled her legs off the arm and sat straight up. "We're still going to that Greek restaurant tonight, though, right? I had to ask Dad to get us a reservation, which is at seven, because *I* tried and since it's so new, they were booked. He had to pull some strings."

"Way to go, Dad!" I cheered, then cringed at my loud voice, damn it. Krystal's dad was a city councilman and knew people and had apparently known someone at the restaurant. "Yes. We're still on." I stood slowly and stretched. "But for now, I think I'm gonna head home, and take a nap."

"You just woke up," she declared with a snort as she stood and took her glass to the kitchen.

"I know. I need a nap from sleeping with a headache." I ran a hand through my tangled hair.

"Wanna do a movie after dinner?" she called.

"Sounds good."

"Oh. Vic called last night," she mentioned, walking back into the living room.

My head shot to her making me wince at the sudden movement and I put a hand to my forehead. "He called you?"

"Well, he called you but since you were passed out, I answered."

"And?"

"He found a window with a broken latch that he thinks Jeremiah came in," she shared.

"Shit. Where?"

"Spare bedroom."

Well, that wasn't horrifying. "Did he fix it?"

"He said he was gonna try to. He also said he called Jeremiah and cussed him out and doubts he'll bother you again." She chuckled.

"Did he say anything about getting an alarm? Wait, what am I saying? More importantly, did you two at least talk?"

She flipped her hair behind her shoulder in annoyance. Great. "He told me he'd like if we could get together sometime and chat." She huffed out a humorless laugh. "Big, bad Victor Justice said *chat*. Can you believe that?" She rolled her eyes and made a *Psh* sound.

I carefully inquired, "So are you gonna talk?"

"Eh. I don't know." She turned and looked at the TV then added offhandedly, "Maybe."

If my head hadn't hurt so bad, I would've let out a squeal. But as it was, I just nodded, biting my lips so I wouldn't smile.

~*~*~*~*~

"Doing anything exciting tonight?" Drake asked when he called around four.

"Krys and I are going to a new restaurant, so I don't know if that classifies as being exciting. Guess if the chef starts juggling his knives it could be," I remarked.

"Honor." His deep voice held a warning.

My brow came down as I wondered what I'd done wrong. "Yeah?"

"You're bein' cute."

"Oh."

"Fuckin' cute." He chuckled low. "Hey, Vic find out how your ex got in?"

"Yes. A window in the spare room had a broken latch," I said, shivering at the thought. "And he's not my ex," I added.

"He fix it?"

"I think so, yeah, but I haven't talked to him today. So, uh, what're you doing tonight?"

"Got some online work for school I've been putting off. Fun, huh?"

"Sounds like a really fun Saturday night. I'll think of you when I'm eating dolmades."

"Don't know what those are and don't think I want to."

I laughed. "They're basically stuffed grape leaves.

"That sounds disgusting."

"They're actually not bad."

"Think I'll stick with my meat and potatoes." He chuckled.

"You do that." I giggled.

"You wanna come by the shop tomorrow afternoon? Gotta transmission I need to work on so I'll be around. My dad called earlier to check on things and said he'd promised the guy it'd be ready Tuesday. I thought since it was Sunday and the garage is closed, I'd have more time, maybe even get it done. Dad said they should be home next Saturday, so depending on what time they get in, maybe I can take you to dinner?"

I'd forgotten his folks were out of town for two weeks. Duh. I mean, we'd just had sandwiches at the garage last night. Oh. And hot sex. I felt a dip in my womb just thinking about it. Gah! But his saying he didn't have evenings free got me thinking.

"Can I ask why you don't have evenings free while they're gone?" I questioned.

"You can."

"Drake."

He laughed. "Because I'm the only one around. I'm responsible for the shop and I don't wanna be too far away."

That made sense. Then I tested, "I could make dinner at your place one night this week."

"Babe."

What was the big deal? Jeez. I let out a breath. "I'll see if I can come by after work tomorrow."

"Good. I wanna see you. Make it happen, babe."

"I'll try," I replied, hurt that he didn't want me at his house.

But after hanging up, I started getting ready for dinner, finding I was excited to go out with Krystal, ready for some quality girl time. I'd showered and now stood looking in my closet not knowing what to pick out.

"Krys," I said into my phone when she answered. "What do I wear?"

"It's Greek to me," she answered with a snort. At my groan, she declared, "Dressy casual. Dark jeans and a nice shirt should do."

"Gotcha."

"Be here in an hour?"

"I can do that. See you then!" I said before hanging up.

CHAPTER 15

"Fancy schmancy," I remarked looking down at the platter of crudités and hummus.

The whole restaurant was gorgeous, very white, very arch-y and very Mediterranean. And the food was almost too pretty to eat. I spooned some hummus onto my plate then used the tongs, nabbing a couple carrots, red peppers and cucumbers.

"Oh, wow. This is amazing," I muttered, crunching on a hummus-dipped carrot.

We chatted as we waited on our main course, which Krystal insisted we both get pastitsio to which I'd agreed to because I was pretty clueless when it came to most Greek foods. We'd also ordered Ouzo, which I hadn't had before but found I could take it or leave it. I mean, nothing says yummy like chasing your food with a drink that tastes like black licorice. Ergh.

"You're the best date I've had in a long time," Krystal said laughing. "Please tell me your ex isn't gonna show up and yell at you for being out with a, and I quote, 'brazen hussy'?"

I snorted. "Honey, if brazen hussy is the worst you've been called, you're doing good."

"I still can't believe Tiffany Green called you a," she leaned in close across the table and whispered, "cunt!" Sitting back, she popped an olive into her mouth and exclaimed, "What a bitch!"

"I can't believe he brought her home," I mumbled. My eyes got big realizing I'd said that out loud which made Krystal chuckle.

"You're fine," she said and took a drink. "Here's the deal, On. I've got it figured out. Vic's looking for someone to replace me. And if Tiffany Green is the best he can do, then I win."

Ah. Just as I figured. But what was ironic was she didn't realize she was doing the same with all the guys she went out with.

"And don't think I don't know I've been doing the same thing with dating." Well, touché. "Except I don't sleep with them."

"If you two'd ever figure out you should be together, you wouldn't have to do all this avoiding each oth—"

"Honor," she interrupted letting me know she didn't want to talk about it.

Instead, we talked a bit about Tiffany and all the girls we'd gone to high school with when just as I was in the middle of telling her that I'd seen Tara Fox at Colonial Manor a few weeks before, Krystal's eyes got huge.

"Honor," she said looking panicked at me. "Do not, and I mean it—listen just this once, Honor—do *not* turn around."

I stared at her for a moment then laughed. "Since when do I ever listen?" I said as I twisted to see what had her in a tizzy.

And I wished I'd listened for a change.

Drake and the stunning blonde who'd yelled at him in the parking lot were walking to be seated a few tables behind us. And I guessed she'd decided to give his masterpiece another go because they looked happy as they went to their table, his hand at the small of her back and when they got there, he pulled the chair out for her to sit.

I whipped my head back to Krystal. "What the actual fuck? That's the same girl I told you about who was screaming at him that day in the parking lot!"

"That's Chanel Chadwick," she stated bitterly, looking past me at their table. "Her dad's one of the top dogs at Amazon. She's a model and has been on runways all over the world—Paris, Berlin, New York, London, Milan."

I knew she had to be a model. Well, wasn't this great. Drake had not only lied about not being available at night or *not fucking around*, he was also dating a fricking runway model! Holy shit.

"What do I do?" I squeaked, angry tears filling my eyes. Then things seemed to be moving in slo-mo—a waiter setting plates on the table next to us, a woman laughing a few tables over, a man holding his fork out for his date to take a bite, all of it just slowed down. "I think I'm gonna pass out."

Krystal's eyes came back to me while she flipped her blond hair behind her shoulder, her jaw getting tight. Then she instructed, "It's just the Ouzo. But here's what's gonna happen, On. You're gonna enjoy your fucking night out with your fucking best friend. You're gonna eat your fucking fantastic food. And you are *not* gonna pass out!" She gave their table a death glare then looked back at me fiercely. "Then we'll fucking figure out what to do." Boy, a hair flip *and* cursing. She was really mad. She picked up my drink holding it out to me. "Finish this. Liquid courage."

"This'll be two nights in a row of drinking heavily, Krys. You know I don't like to drink." I frowned taking the glass from her anyway. When raising my brow at her caused a random tear to slip down my cheek, I wiped it away angrily. "You're making me have mixed drinks about my feelings."

She laughed. "I fucking love you, you know that, right? And the fact that you can hold your shit together by making a joke right now goes to show how truly fucking amazing you are."

"I love you too. And you only think I'm amazing 'cause I'm doing what you're telling me to do," I replied before downing my drink and making a face. "Why couldn't the Greeks have invented strawberry daiquiris?" I gasped with a shudder. She was watching their table again. "What're they doing now?"

"She just laughed at something he said. Now I'm assuming the waitress is taking their drink orders."

At that moment, our waiter brought our food, all cheery and shit. Krystal ordered me another drink at which I started to protest then thought, why the hell not? It was going to be a painful night for me as it was; I may as well be smashed.

"This is great," she muttered as she chewed.

But all I could do was stare down at my plate until, on her insistence, I took a bite but couldn't really taste anything, either because I was numb or my taste buds had been positively obliterated by the alcohol. So while she ate, I drank, pondering why in the world I'd thought Drake and I had had something anyway. He'd been keeping things from me—no telling how many secrets he had—which made me see that he neither trusted me nor had ever planned on getting serious with me to begin with.

"I'm an idiot," I murmured, drinking my Ouzo and still scrunching up my face at its taste. "Fuck. You mean to tell me eleven million people love this shit?" I asked as a tremor ran through me.

"You're not an idiot. He's an asshole. And eleven million people can't be wrong," she pointed out with a chuckle. "Keep drinking until you feel like you can face him."

And I did, not only finishing my glass but the rest of hers too. A few minutes later, I sat back and giggled out an, "I don't feel a thing."

"You're ready," she proclaimed.

"Yep," I agreed, and don't think I didn't pop the hell out of that *P*.

"Can we get boxes, please?" Krystal asked a waiter who was passing our table. When the server left, she turned to me. "What are you gonna say?"

"I don't know," my bravado suddenly taking a hit when I realized this was really going to happen. "I just wanna go home and sleep forever," I whispered, slumping down into my chair.

"He's not getting away with this, On. You're gonna confront him. Make him explain. Then you can go home and sleep. Okay?"

I looked at her for a moment seeing the determination on her face which infused me with some of my own. Sitting up, I nodded. Then, because alcohol, I stipulated with a giggle, "But not until I throw a glass of water in his face."

"Perfect!"

Our waiter came back and boxed our food. After we paid the check, I turned in my chair and watched as Chanel said something that made Drake laugh and she reached a hand across the table to squeeze his.

"Get mad, Honor," Krystal urged.

"Oh, don't worry. I'm mad," I said. Gathering my mettle, I stood to leave, instantly feeling the full effects of the liquor, except this time my anger had my adrenaline spiking so I was more pissy than giggly. Between my nerves and the liquor, my legs wobbled a little as I began my trek over to where they sat.

As I approached their table, all I could think about was that he'd lied to me about not being able to go out in the evening while his folks were gone, lied that he didn't fuck around, lied about...everything. Just flat-out lied. And tonight? Online work, my ass.

I was halfway there, my heart thundering so hard in my chest I again thought I was going to pass the fuck out before I even got to them, when I scolded myself, muttering, "Breathe, Honor!" Glancing behind me, I saw Krystal right there with me and instantly calmed down.

Drake and Ms. Runway were looking at their menus when I stopped at the table, and he must've thought I was the waitress because he said, "I think we'll start out with the tzatziki and pita crisps."

"Can I get you some dolmades too?" I asked, actually kind of getting a kick out of watching his head come up and seeing the shock on his face when he saw it was me.

"Honor," he said pushing his chair back and standing. "What're you doing here?"

"Oh, just having that exciting time we talked about earlier," I replied, proud of myself for keeping my voice from shaking.

We stood looking at each other for a few seconds until I raised my eyebrows darting my eyes to his date then back to him.

"Oh. Uh, Honor Justice, this is Cha—"

"Chanel Chadwick," I finished for him, glancing down at her and faux smiling. "I'm a big fan," I added insincerely.

She looked me up and down, apparently unimpressed as she uttered, "Oh, really?"

Turning back to Drake, I waited for his explanation, again proud of the indifference I was displaying. And viva la fucking Ouzo.

He leaned down to me and said low, "It's not what you think."

"It's not? You're not having dinner with a runway model? I mean," I poked him in the chest, "I'm sure *you're* going to eat." I next looked down at Chanel. "But you probably won't. Or can't. Or if you do, I'm willing to bet that tzatziki will be making an appearance in Ladies Restroom Stall Number Three in the next thirty minutes. Am I right?" I gave her another fake smile as she narrowed her eyes at me.

"Honor, stop," Drake warned.

My head snapped up so fast, I saw him flinch. "Don't you fucking tell me to stop," I hissed, my anger clearly guiding me now. "Don't fucking tell me anything ever again." Grabbing his glass of what I hoped was water from the table, I threw it in his face. When I realized it was Ouzo, I snorted. "Ouzo for the fucking win." I looked at Krystal. "Ready?"

"Absolutely," she said, giving them both a hard glower before hooking her arm in mine and pulling me with her.

Ignoring not only the hubbub that was going on behind us since Drake's waiter had rushed up with a towel to help him clean up, but also the stares of the other patrons, I mumbled, "Guess we won't be welcome back here again, huh?"

Krystal laughed. "It wasn't that good anyway. I've had way better...at Petra downtown!" she said loudly enough so the wait staff and host could hear not to mention the customers waiting to be seated. We didn't even try to contain our giggles at the staff's gasps as we made our way outside where she handed the valet her ticket.

"Did Chanel seem like a snob?" I asked Krystal as we waited on her car. "She seemed snobby."

She huffed out a laugh. "Definitely."

"And what do you think Drake meant by it wasn't what I thought?"

Her car appeared and we got in.

"I don't know. He can explain later," she replied putting her seatbelt on. "But he so deserved all of that," she added as we drove off.

My anger high was waning and I started feeling drowsy. Resting my head back against the seat I revealed, "You know, I don't even feel bad."

"You shouldn't."

"Gonna buy me a case of that stuff and stay drunk all the time 'cause I have no fucks to give at all right now."

She chuckled. "Now there's a plan."

"Yeah, well, it sure beats the hell out of crying," I muttered, closing my eyes.

"You're coming home with me so you're not alone," she stated.

"Sometimes it's better to be alone..."

"On," she mildly scolded my using a Megara line.

"That way nobody can hurt you," I paraphrased before drifting off.

CHAPTER 16

"Ouzo is the devil," I mumbled the next morning. I'd put my phone on speaker when Krystal called. I was still in bed and lay on my stomach with a pillow over my head to block any sunlight that might've even thought about coming in through my blinds, my phone under the pillow with me.

"So I need to cancel the case of it I ordered for you?" she retorted.

I tried rolling my eyes but stopped because it hurt too much. "I'm never drinking again."

"It's my fault. I made you drink both times," she confessed.

"You're a bad influence."

She chuckled. "You're just figuring this out after ten years?"

I let out a grumble as I pulled the pillow down more tightly. "How'd I get home?" I asked.

"You don't remember telling me we wouldn't be best friends anymore if I didn't take you home?"

"God," I groaned. "Now we know Ouzo makes me bitchy."

She chuckled. "Apparently. So, have you heard from Drake?"

"Ugh. I don't want to talk about it this early," I whined.

"On, it's eleven-thirty."

"That's like five a.m. in alcohol time," I groused.

But I knew he'd tried contacting me. He'd called five times and texted ten. I was also fairly sure he'd even come by the house this morning, but I'd felt like crap—and knew I definitely looked it—and hadn't answered the door which was when I'd checked my phone to see the missed calls and texts.

When I told Krystal this, she said, "You *are* gonna talk to him, right?"

"Yes. When I don't feel like dog shit."

"Okay. Let me know how it goes."

"I will. Thanks for getting my drunk ass home."

"You'd do the same for me."

"I would and have," I said snorting then letting out a groan.

"Call me later."

After hanging up, I slept for another hour, my poor body and brain needing to recover from two freaking nights in a row of consuming liquor. Yuck. When I finally got up, I showered, ate some toast, drank what was probably the equivalent of a gallon of water and felt much better.

Then it was time to face the music. Ergh.

Grabbing my phone, I saw I had a missed call from Drake just after 11 last night—and four others this morning—and even though I'd seen his text messages earlier I hadn't exactly been sober enough to read them which I now decided to do.

Text Message—Sat, Mar 19, 11:09 p.m.

Drake: Answer your phone

Drake: Honor, pick up

Drake: It's not what you think

Drake: Fuck! Call me

Text Message—Sun, Mar 20, 6:09 a.m.

Drake: I'm coming by

Drake: Answer your door

Drake: Honor

Drake: Call me later

Drake: I'm at the garage if you wanna come by

Drake: Fuck

Huh.

I sat at the table staring at my phone when Victor came into the kitchen wearing only the blue and black plaid, flannel sleeping pants I'd gotten him for Christmas and rubbing his hands over his face.

"Got anything good to eat?" he asked, heading to the fridge and pulling out the milk.

"There are some chocolate chip cookies I made in the jar." I turned and caught him just as he was about to drink the milk from the container and scolded, "Victor Edward Justice! You stop right now!"

He pulled the carton away from his mouth, grinning as he walked to the cabinet to retrieve a glass and fill it.

"You'd better not be doing that when I'm not here. Gross! I use a lot of milk in baking and I don't want your germs in everything." I made a face which made him chuckle.

Clutching the cookie jar under his elbow against his side, he brought it and his glass to the table and sat across from me. "I don't do it all the time, On." He pulled out a cookie eating it in two bites. "Fuck, these are good."

"Thanks." I gave him a look as I added, "And please don't do it *any* time. It's disgusting."

"Found out some bad news," he said, mouth full.

I looked up from my phone. "What?"

"Finch just told me last night that someone's skimming the till." At my shocked look, he continued. "He said almost ten grand was taken last year." My mouth fell open at what his boss had told him as he took a drink of milk. "And almost two thousand so far this year."

"Twelve thousand total? Good grief. Does he have any idea who it is?" I asked.

He shrugged. "I've always been suspicious of Ingram. He started working last March which is around the time it began."

"Damn."

"Yeah." He looked at me as he chewed another cookie. "So what's wrong?"

My eyes narrowed. "How do you know something's wrong?"

"When you're upset, you get those little lines between your eyes." He put his fingers just above the bridge of his nose to show me where.

Great. Wrinkles. I used my thumb and forefinger to smooth out the lines and blew out a breath. "Krys and I went to eat at this new restaurant last night." I bit my lips before saying, "Drake was there with another woman."

He frowned as he took a drink. "You two exclusive?" he asked after setting the glass down.

I shrugged. "He told me he doesn't fuck around, whatever that means."

"You talk to him?"

"I confronted him, yeah."

"And?"

Another sigh. "He said it wasn't what I thought."

Now he shrugged. "Then trust him."

I let out an unamused huff. "Sure. He's out with a model and I'm supposed to trust him. I'll get right on that."

Vic's eyebrows came up. "Model?"

"Chanel Chadwick." He shook his head not recognizing the name. "Her dad's some big shot at Amazon. She's a runway model, Krys said. Travels all over the world."

"Never heard of her," he claimed.

We sat in silence as I put my hands in my lap and leaned against the table putting my forehead on it. "I may also have thrown a glass of Ouzo in his face."

"Fuck." He snorted. After a couple minutes, he asked, "You heard from him since?"

"He's texted and called. And he came by the house this morning but I was too busy being not sober to answer it."

"He must have it bad for you then," he mumbled.

"Why do you say that?" I asked raising my head from the table to look at my brother. I mean, Drake had been out with another woman! If that wasn't a blatant statement of not having it bad for me, I didn't know what was.

"If he didn't care, he wouldn't have bothered."

I stared at him. "You think I should talk to him?"

"Up to you," he replied. He stood and went to the sink to rinse his glass out.

Watching as he came back for the cookie jar, I questioned, "Do you keep secrets from girls you're serious about?"

He placed the jar on the counter and turned, leaning back against it, crossing his arms over his bare chest. "Depends."

"What's that mean?"

"If I robbed a bank and wasn't sure how she'd handle that bit of info, I'd probably keep it to myself."

I rolled my eyes. "Get serious."

"Like I said, it depends."

"Have there been times when you didn't want a woman to come to the house?"

He laughed. "Plenty."

"Why?" I questioned as my brow came down.

He pushed off the counter with his butt. "If they're crazy, I don't want them to know where I fucking live."

"So Drake thinks I'm crazy..."

Walking behind me, he grabbed the messy bun on top of my head and shook it. "Not saying that, On. Talk to him and I'm sure he'll explain," he offered, leaving the kitchen then calling from the hallway, "Gotta go in early! Taking a shower and I'm outta here! And make some more of those fucking awesome cookies!"

~*~*~*~*~

By four o'clock, I'd succeeded in taking up two hours after Vic left by cleaning out the fridge first then making cookies.

And avoiding calling Drake.

Just as I pulled the last batch out of the oven, the doorbell rang.

Wiping my hands on a towel on the way into the living room, I peeked out the front window then proceeded to suck in so much air that I choked.

Drake!

Crap!

My coughing finally under control, I cleared my throat, biting my lower lip not knowing what to do. Let's see, be an adult or keep running from this like a baby. Hm. What to do.

"I know you're in there, Honor. Saw your truck," he called through the door. Then he tacked on, "And heard you coughing."

Damn it.

All right. Adulting it was.

I opened the front door and looked at him dispassionately through the storm door raising my eyebrows.

"Can I come in?" he grated out, having the nerve to look offended that I hadn't just welcomed him in all chipper and shit.

Now chewing the inside of my lip in indecision—and giving him one hell of an apathetic look of which I was proud because he looked so good I wanted to jump on him and have my way with him until I remembered he'd been on a friggin' date the night before—deeeeep breath—I finally unlocked the screen door with an annoyed huff letting him in.

I turned my back and walked into the living room as he shut the door. Then facing him, I crossed my arms over my chest and questioned, "What do you want, Drake?"

His hands went to his hips as he exhaled through his nose. "Last night isn't what you're thinking."

I raised an eyebrow. "Really? It looked like a date to me."

He shook his head. "That's not what it was."

"Are you sleeping with her?"

"No. Told you I don't fuck around."

"What was it then?"

His head went back and he stared at the ceiling for a long moment. Then looking at me again, he repeated, "It wasn't a date."

Irked at that non-answer answer, I remarked, "See? That's what I've been talking about. You keep things from me because you don't trust me." Puffing out a humorless laugh, I continued. "But I figured it out last night. *This*," I flashed a finger several times between us, "is nothing serious to you."

Hands still on his hips, his face suddenly broke into a grin—which might've just pissed me right the hell off just then—and he lowered and shook his head at the floor, chuckling. "Whatever you wanna think, Honor." His head came up and he declared, "This is very fucking serious to me." He took a step toward me. "And it wasn't a date," he reiterated.

"You lied about having to stay home," I pointed out.

He stopped in his tracks, eyes narrowing. "I didn't lie. Something came up which meant fuck all to me but I had to go along."

I frowned and shook my head. "What does that even mean?"

"It means it wasn't a date," he answered, taking another step.

"Oh, no you don't," I warned, holding a palm out toward him and taking a step back. "Stop, Drake."

He smirked as he kept moving forward.

"I can't be with you if you don't trust me," I stated, my back hitting the wall just at the hall entrance.

Before I could move away, he was there, hands on either side of me trapping me in. Leaning down and locking eyes with me, he stated cryptically, "I just have to be sure."

"You keep saying that. What the hell does it me—" His mouth smashed down onto mine before I could finish.

And, good lord, I loved the way he kissed. As a consequence, I couldn't not kiss him back because I was still so freaking attracted to him. Our mouths still connected, he pulled the band from my hair while at the same time backing me down the hallway toward my bedroom, which I knew was a bad idea and at which I tried putting on the brakes. Okay, it would've been a totally amazing idea and "tried" is probably too strong a word for what I actually did, but whatever. But once inside my room, putting my hands to his chest, I *did* push off and back way the hell away from him as he shut the door.

"We're not doing this, Drake," I said when he turned, eyes hot on me.

"We are. Believe what you wanna believe about last night, Honor, but I'm telling you the truth. It wasn't a date."

He'd said that numerous times, but I still didn't know if I was convinced. I mean, I'd seen him out with another woman! What more could it have been? I now stood staring at him, my brain still trying to catch up in the letting-my-body-know-this-wasn't-going-to-happen-between-us department when I heard a click as he locked my door and a shiver ran through me.

Guess my body didn't get the memo.

His eyes stayed on mine as he removed the flannel shirt he wore then he reached behind his head to pull off his very freaking cool Slipknot t-shirt—leave it to me to notice stupid shit like that—and holy damn. That chest. Those abs. And those colorful, gorgeous hot tattoos. My body was already in an aroused state just from kissing and now watching him disrobe.

As I stood there thinking how badly I wanted him but knowing I probably shouldn't, I decided right then I was a grown-assed woman and if I wanted to fuck him, I would. I mean, hello, sexy man undressing in front of me? Hell yes. I'd deal with the emotional fallout later, but right then, I didn't care.

Eyes flashing at mine as if daring me, he gave me a barely detectable nod and I knew he wanted me to take off my shirt too.

Since I'd never been one to back down from a dare, I pulled off my shirt, standing there in my bra, jeans and sock-covered feet, raising my brow all, "What now?"

I saw his lip twitch the smallest bit then his hands went to his jeans, unbuttoning them.

Another small nod from him had me undoing my own jeans after which I again gave him an indifferent look.

This went on until he was down to just his boxer briefs and me to my panties and bra when his head made another slight movement, his eyes going to the floor then back to mine.

I narrowed mine at what he was suggesting.

God.

God!

I knew now this was nothing but a power play. He was testing to see if *I* trusted *him*.

Because up until now, I'd been the one asking for his trust, but he was presently showing me that I hadn't given him my own, not really. As I stood there, chest heaving with my breaths, trying to decide if I could go there, it felt as if this moment was huge, monumental as to what would happen between us in what I'd do next.

Heart pounding in my chest, I lifted my chin the tiniest bit, showing that I was making the decision to trust, before slowly dropping to my knees for him, resting my butt down on my calves.

I saw his eyes crinkle a little at the sides; he was pleased.

"Good girl," he pronounced, voice husky with lust. He slowly stalked toward me moving to where I knelt.

Watching him, I found myself unsure, uncertain of going forward with this. I'd given him my trust but now would he give me his? He'd kept saying he had to be sure but I was still clueless as to what that meant.

He now stood in front of me, his hard cock straining against his boxer briefs, his eyes piercing mine as he looked down. Reaching a hand down and cupping the side of my face, he languidly ran his thumb over my bottom lip.

"So fucking beautiful," he remarked, watching the movement his thumb made.

Then his eyes locked on mine, the gleam in his silently communicating something I wasn't quite grasping, but when he knelt too, I sucked in a breath.

His voice was low and gravelly when he uttered, "Give me time."

He wasn't asking; he was telling. But he was trying.

I nodded which generated a slow smirk from him.

Abruptly, he grabbed me by the waist, pulling me up onto my knees and kissed me before his mouth veered away to leave soft kisses at the side of my neck while his hands dropped to tug my panties down and off.

From somewhere he produced a condom, and suddenly his briefs were down and he'd covered his thick shaft with it. He next lifted me to straddle him and slowly slid me down to sheath his cock.

"Oh, my God," I whispered, hands on his shoulders, my head falling back as I took all of him inside.

His lips landed back on my neck where he peppered it with gentle kisses, his hands at my waist holding me steady as his hips moved up in deliberate and measured thrusts that already had my climax building.

"Love how fucking wet you get for me, Honor..." he said, his breath hot on my skin.

Brushing his lips down, he kissed between my breasts before moving to one, his hand coming up to pull my bra aside then he sucked my nipple into his mouth causing me to let out a throaty moan.

Lips gliding across to my other breast, he gave it the same attention as the other, and it was then I realized this wasn't like the other times we'd been together—hard and rough, unrestrained fucking; no, this was slow and calculated with a bit of tender thrown in. He was giving me soft and sweet—he was making love to me.

At this thought, I tipped over the edge, my body completely giving in, my amplified arousal escalating into a mind-blowing orgasm. Digging my fingers into his shoulders, my head came forward and I cried out his name. Then he was there too, his hips moving faster as he wrapped his arms tightly around me, and pushing his hips up hard he buried himself deep with a groan. We stayed locked in each other's arms for a long time, as if our bodies needed the closeness, our minds the assurance of the other.

When he pulled back, he touched his lips to mine and said low, "You're one of the best fucking things in my life." He then kissed my forehead and as he lifted me off him, his lips brushing my mouth again before moving down between my breasts, over my belly and finally to my thigh as I stood. "Time," he uttered looking up at me. It was now more of a question than a statement as it had been before.

Gazing down at him still kneeling before me, his eyes almost pleading with me, I felt my insides go to mush. "Okay," I whispered back.

And I *was* okay. He'd said it wasn't a date, so I knew I had to trust. And obviously, something had happened to him that made it hard for him to trust, so I decided to give him time.

I just hoped it didn't take too long.

CHAPTER 17

Drake left around seven after looking at the time on his phone and groaning out a, "Fuck."

We'd talked a bit more after we'd dressed, sitting on my bed where he'd pulled me sideways onto his lap.

"I know I'm keeping things from you, but I fucking promise, if we last, I'll tell you everything."

"Can you at least tell me—"

"I promise," he interrupted so I guessed I was finished questioning him. He'd kissed me sweetly then said, "Gotta get back, babe. Can you come by the garage Tuesday night?"

"Maybe," I answered, giving him a smirk as he nudged me to stand.

"Do it," he replied, bending to touch his lips to mine. "Not gonna be very available this week. Everyone's busy and Mom and Dad won't be back until this weekend. But I want to see you. If I could come here, I would but it's just not feasible. Sorry."

It made me wonder why it wasn't feasible, but I'd told myself I'd trust him, so I commented, "I'll see what I can do."

After he left, I made myself a sandwich, did some homework then went to bed.

~*~*~*~*~

Monday was the same as usual—school, work, home.

But Drake and I had texted throughout the day, which was different. He usually only called or texted me at night, but I wasn't complaining. I liked staying in contact with him and it let me know he was thinking about me.

He called at ten just as I was lying down for bed.

"Hey," I answered.

"Hey, beautiful. Calling to let you know I miss you."

I let out a dreamy sigh. "I miss you too."

"What're you doing?"

"Just got in bed."

"Mm. What're you wearing?" he asked, voice low and gruff.

I chuckled. "Same thing as usual—tank top and shorts."

"Fuck. I want you in my bed..." he trailed off.

I sat up on my elbow. "You know, I could come over, Drake."

I heard him groan. "Not tonight, baby."

God. This trusting thing was so difficult. "Okay," I whispered, lying back down.

"Just don't wanna drag you into everything," he stated.

This was new. "Drag me into what?"

"I just need to be sure," he said for what had to be at least the third time.

"Sure of what?" He was so damned secretive. Ugh.

"But you know what?"

"What?"

"If I was there, my mouth would be on your sweet pussy," he shared, instantly making my womb dip.

"Drake…" I said quietly.

"Touch yourself, Honor," he instructed. When I didn't reply, he ordered, "Do it."

"Okay," I said, letting out a small gasp when I felt myself already slick for him.

"You wet, baby?"

"Yes…"

"Fuck…" he rasped. "Think of my tongue on you…in you…sucking your clit inside my mouth."

"Oh, God," I moaned, my body trembling as my fingers moved.

"Want you to come, baby…put a finger inside…"

I did as he said, feeling my body getting hotter, my back arching off the bed as I was just on the verge of climaxing.

"Hearing you, picturing you…is making me so hard…Christ," he ground out.

"Drake!" I cried as I gave in to my orgasm which left me shuddering and breathless. Damn.

"You make me want you so fucking bad…"

"I want you too…" I breathed.

"Fuck…"

As I came back to myself, I asked, "You could come over…"

I heard him let out a breath. "Time, babe…" When I stayed quiet, he said, "Gonna let you go. I'll talk to you tomorrow, baby."

We hung up and even though my body was in a state of bliss, my mind was questioning everything and I fell into a fitful sleep.

~*~*~*~*~

Voices coming from the living room woke me and I lay there listening wondering if I'd just been dreaming.

"You stole the money, asshole!" I heard a man yell and sat up immediately, heart in my throat as I grabbed my phone to see that it was just after two in the morning.

"You're a goddamned liar," Vic replied. "Albert's setting me up! This is all his shit right here!"

Albert? As in our stepdad? What the hell?

I got out of bed and opened my door quietly, peeking down the hall to see Vic in the living room with two other men.

"Oh, yeah? Then who took the ten grand? Huh?" one of the men asked.

"I don't fucking know but it wasn't me!" Vic answered.

"Vic?" I called as I stepped out into the hallway.

In a clipped voice and not looking at me, he demanded, "Go back to bed, Honor."

"Want me to call the police?" I asked.

His head jerked toward me. "No! Go back to bed!"

I stood there in my pjs shuddering when the two men turned and gave me lurid looks.

"Let her join the party, Justice. We could make a deal here," one of the men said with a nasty grin.

Turning his head to the guy, Vic bit out, "Fuck you!" The men laughed as my brother looked back at me, pure fury on his face. "Go back in your room and lock the fucking door! Now!" Vic told me.

I spun and went into my room contemplating on whether I should call the police or not. Not knowing what else to do, I called Drake.

"Yeah," I heard him answer sleepily.

"Drake!" I whispered. "There are two men in the house with Vic and I don't know what to do!"

"Honor?" I heard him moving around before he came back on the line. "What's going on?"

"They're yelling saying he took money."

"Who is it?"

"I don't know. I heard yelling and looked in the living room. Two guys are in there with him."

"Hang up and call the police then call me back."

"Vic told me not to call the police!"

"Fuck!"

"What if they hurt him?" I said as I heard more yelling from the front room.

"Call 911 and stay in your room!"

"But he told me not to call," I repeated, feeling the tears well up in my eyes. "I'm scared, Drake. Can you come here?"

I heard him curse low. "I'll try, Honor."

"What?" I whispered, shocked that he wouldn't say he'd be here.

"I'm sorry, baby. I can't just leave."

Huh. When I heard a loud crash from the living room, I let out a gasp.

"Call 911, Honor! Now!"

"O-okay," I said hanging up then dialing the police. The dispatcher came on the line and when I told her what was going on, she said they'd send a car over immediately.

After disconnecting, I ran out of my room and across the hall to Vic's to grab his baseball bat. "I called the cops!" I yelled, running into the living room to see my brother with a bloody face and the coffee table smashed to pieces. Screaming, "Get the fuck out of our house!" I swung the bat at the nearest man who moved easily out of the way with a laugh.

"Call off your bodyguard, Justice," he said with a chuckle then looking at the other guy, he nodded toward the door.

I swung at the other man who grabbed the bat right from my hands. "Sassy little thing, aren't you?" he said with a sneer.

"Get out!" I yelled.

He grinned then threw the bat on the floor as he headed to the front door. Turning, he told Vic, "You have until Friday to pay everything back."

"Fuck you!" my brother shouted just as they slammed the door behind them.

Now a sobbing mess, I went to Vic. "Are y-you o-okay?"

"I'm fine," he assured me, going to the kitchen and flipping on the light.

I followed him to the sink, watching as he spit blood then splashed water on his face. I handed him a hand towel that he used to pat his face dry.

"Do y-you need stitches?" I choked out, looking at the nasty cut below his eye. He shook his head and I questioned, "Wh-who were they?"

"Just some assholes."

"But I heard you say something about Albert?"

There was a rap at the front door and a man called, "Police!"

My brother now glared at me. "I didn't call them!" I cried.

Wiping my eyes, I went to answer the door but he cut me off with his body. "Go to bed."

I stared at his back as he walked to the front door, wondering what in the world was going on.

When he looked over his shoulder seeing that I hadn't immediately done as he said, he bit out just as he reached for the doorknob, "I'd probably fuckin' die if you ever fuckin' listened, Honor."

I scowled as a few tears ran down my cheeks then giving in, went to my room but kept my door cracked standing at it and listening to the police questioning him about what happened.

"It was two guys who thought they knew me," Vic explained.

"The call came from a woman. She here?" one of the officers asked.

At that, I stepped out of my room and went into the living room. "I called."

"Are you okay?" the other officer inquired looking me over for injuries.

I nodded.

"And you say you don't know who they were?" the first cop asked Vic, looking at him suspiciously.

Vic shook his head.

"And you don't wanna file a report?"

Another head shake.

The second cop looked at the bat first, then the broken table before looking at me. I wondered if he thought Vic and I had gotten in a fight and we were now lying. Then he told his partner, "Nothing we can do here then."

The first cop studied Vic for a long moment. "You sure?"

My brother nodded.

"All right," the officer said giving up and going to the door. "Make sure to lock up," he suggested before they left.

Vic locked the door behind them and turned to face me. "I know Albert set this shit up. Ingram's probably a plant he's put in the bar to frame me."

I sucked in a breath at hearing that. "What? Why?"

He let out a huff. "Payback."

My phone rang from my room but I ignored it. "Payback? Seriously? After all this time?"

Once again, I followed him to the kitchen watching as he rinsed out the towel in the sink then got ice from the fridge and put in it. Holding the towel against the cut under his eye, he disclosed, "I didn't think he'd do anything but I guess the fucker has some balls after all."

"What're we gonna do?"

"*We're* not gonna do anything," he informed me. "I'll take care of it."

"How?"

"Don't worry about it."

I frowned. "I *will* worry about it!"

My phone rang again and again I ignored it.

"I'll talk to Finch tomorrow. Let him know it's not me." He let out a breath. "Go to bed, On."

"Did those guys follow you home?" I asked.

He looked at the floor and shook his head. "They broke in."

"How?" We'd had two break-ins now? God.

"When I got home, they came out of the spare room." My mouth dropped open. "I know. I'm sorry. I was gonna fix the fucking lock tomorrow."

Oh, my God.

Oh, my God!

"Th-they were in the house when I was alone?" I shrieked. I didn't think my nerves could have gotten any more rattled than what they already were, but upon hearing they'd been in the house with me, well, they definitely did.

"I'm sorry."

Shit!

"And you didn't tell the police they broke in?" I screamed.

"I said I'm sorry, Honor."

I stared at Vic for several moments, completely unnerved, then whispered, "Please fix it now." When my phone rang again, I left the kitchen and walked to my room on shaky legs. My phone was on my bed and I sat down seeing it was Drake calling. "Hello?"

"Are you okay?" he yelled. "You didn't pick up!"

I sniffed then realized I was kind of pissed that he hadn't come over when I'd asked and now found myself being a bit snippy at his concern.

"I'm fine. We're fine."

"Tell Vic I called the police because I was worried about you," he disclosed. "So what happened?"

After taking a breath and blowing it out, trying to get hold of myself, I told him, "Two guys broke in saying Vic stole money from the bar. They left before the police got here. But Vic didn't wanna file charges and that's pretty much it."

"Damn. I had to make some calls but I'm on my way—"

"No, it's okay. You don't have to come over," I interrupted.

"I'm sorry I couldn't be there sooner. I'll be there in a few minutes," he said, hanging up before I could tell him to go back.

I'd heard Vic go into his room, so I now went across the hall and knocked quietly on his door.

"What?" he called.

When he opened the door and I looked up to see the cut under his left eye again, I couldn't help the fresh tears that filled my eyes. "Are you sure you're gonna be okay?"

"Yeah."

"What if they come back? Or find you somewhere else and really hurt you?"

He sighed then came to me wrapping his arms around me in a hug. "It's not gonna happen, On. I know Albert's behind this. He just wants us scared. But I'll get to the bottom of it, okay?" He kissed the top of my head and letting me go, looked down at me, eyebrows raised waiting for confirmation.

My brow wrinkled with worry. "Okay. But, please, Vic. If something else happens, please let the police handle it."

He nodded.

"Promise?" I asked.

"Yep."

I didn't believe him but knew it was no use in arguing. "Drake's coming by. You good with it?"

"Yeah," he mumbled.

"I'm gonna put some clothes on," I said. Instead of going across to my room, I went into the bathroom because I needed a flipping moment.

I sat on the edge of the tub, my nerves still shattered at the thought of the men breaking into our house. If they'd wanted, they could've hurt me. They *had* hurt Vic and could've done a lot more to him. Then I'd come out swinging a fucking bat—while they were probably carrying guns—of which they'd easily disarmed me. I let out a shuddering gasp before standing and going to the sink. After splashing cold water on my face and drying it, I went to my room.

While pulling on a pair of jeans and a hoodie, I heard Vic answer the front door.

"Fuck. You okay, man?" Drake asked.

"I'm good," I heard Vic reply as I went back to the bathroom to freshen up.

"What the fuck happened?" Drake said.

I didn't hear what else was said but when I came out, I heard Vic saying, "—getting me back from when he tried hitting on my sister."

I walked into the living room and Drake's eyes hit mine, instantly narrowing. "Explain."

"Sick fuck walked in on her while she showered. I beat him up then put up some flyers calling him a pedophile." Vic snorted. "He said he'd get me back, so I guess that's what this is."

"Fuck," Drake muttered, eyes still on me.

"Hey," I said, going over to him.

"Hey, baby." He bent and wrapped his arms around my waist, picking me up and kissing me. "I'm glad you're okay," he said when he pulled away looking me over before putting me down.

"I'm fine," I confirmed, a little embarrassed that Vic was there to see that.

"Gonna go fix that fucking window," my brother said.

"Need any help?" Drake asked.

"Nah. But thanks."

When we were alone, Drake took my hand and led me to the couch where we sat.

"Tell me about this stepdad."

"Tell me why you had to make some calls before you could get here," I countered.

"Honor..."

Huffing out a breath I said, "Why should I tell you everything when you tell me nothing?"

I watched him purse his lips in aggravation.

"Uh huh. That's what I thought," I murmured, realizing I was tired and gripy, my adrenaline now having suddenly crashed and we probably shouldn't have been having that conversation right then. But I was annoyed that he felt I should be so open while he held back.

"I didn't come here to fight," he murmured.

"Yeah," I replied with a sigh. "Look. I appreciate your coming over but I've got class in the morning and I know you have to work."

He nodded slowly, staring at a place on the wall and I knew he was pissed off, but whatever. I still didn't know who the woman was he'd been out with or who Will was. And to me, it all just seemed like kind of a deal breaker at this point.

"Yeah," he echoed then stood and walked to the front door.

"Goodnight, Drake," I said, tiptoeing up and touching my lips to his, which by the way weren't very responsive.

"'Night, Honor," he said and left.

It took me an hour to settle down as I lay in bed listening to Vic repairing the window, completely disturbed that the men had been in the house with me and I hadn't even known it. I also wondered why Drake wouldn't open up to me and let me in.

I drifted off just as sunlight filled my room.

CHAPTER 18

I noticed Victor had cleaned up the ruined coffee table when I got up a few hours later, and I shivered remembering what'd happened.

Making the strongest pot of coffee I could, I poured it into a travel mug then headed to class. But even after downing most of the caffeinated java on the way, I found I could barely keep my eyes open as I tried taking notes. The classroom had been so cozy and the professor had droned on and on it seemed, and I was soon nodding off.

After class as I drove to Colonial Manor, I called Krystal to tell her what had happened the night before.

"What? Oh, my God! They were in the house with you? That's so scary! Are you okay?" she cried.

"Yes, and it was scary as hell, Krys. Vic has a huge cut under his eye."

"Oh, no! Is he okay?"

"I think so. I thought he might need stitches, but, of course, he wouldn't get them."

"God. I'm so sorry, honey. I'm glad you're okay."

"Me too. Hopefully, he'll get things cleared up with his boss and those guys will leave him alone."

"I'm gonna call him," she declared.

I smiled huge but tried to keep the happiness out of my voice so as not to spook her. "Yeah. That'd probably be good."

We hung up and I let out a squeal just because I could, saying a quick prayer that they'd get back together just as I pulled up to the nursing home.

After clocking in, I helped Alex change a few patients and make a couple beds before it was time to get the meds ready. When I got to Mrs. Johnson's room, she was her usual crabby self.

"Holly. You look terrible. Didn't you get enough sleep last night?" she chided as I handed her the medicine cup.

"No, sorry, Aunt Greta. We had some excitement early this morning," I replied, now handing her water.

She looked up at me. "A young woman always needs to look her best. How do you think you'll get Robert to propose looking this way?"

I rolled my eyes at her old-fashioned notions as she swallowed her pills with the water.

"Don't you roll your eyes at me, young lady."

Damn. She didn't miss anything. "Sorry, Aunt Greta," I said as I took her cups and threw them away.

"Love is a funny thing, dear. I know I'm always getting onto you about the way you look, but you have a beautiful heart, and if Robert doesn't appreciate that, well, he can just go...jump off a cliff!" She let out a Hmph! which made me chuckle.

"Thank you," I said as I pushed the cart to the door. "I'll see you tomorrow?"

"You will," she stated firmly. "In the meantime, don't you worry about a thing. If he's not smart enough to let you in, then you need to just move along. Do you hear me?"

I raised my eyebrows at her sage advice. "I hear you. Have a good night."

As I passed Mr. Avery's old room, I let out a sigh, glancing in and smiling at the new resident who'd moved in. He didn't need meds during my shift, so I kept going, making my way to the last two rooms.

After work, I thought about going by the garage to see Drake but decided against it. I knew we'd left things kind of up in the air, but I felt the ball was in his court now. And Mrs. Johnson's words had struck a chord with me. Drake hadn't let me in, so maybe I should move on. I mean, he kept telling me he had to be sure, but I felt that I'd proven to him that I was trustworthy and hadn't given him a reason not to be sure. Well, except for maybe being sort of bitchy to him last night, but I felt as if that was warranted. At this point, I didn't know what he wanted. And maybe I wasn't the one who could give him what he wanted anyway.

Although it broke my heart, I decided as I pulled into my drive that maybe we weren't meant to be. And I was just going to have to find a way to be okay with that.

~*~*~*~*~

Tuesday night, I did go by the garage to see if we could talk but it was closed up tight.

Same on Wednesday night.

Thursday evening when I drove by, Drake was outside talking to a blond woman who had her back to me, and I was pretty sure it was Chanel. When I saw her Porsche, I knew it was her. Hoping he hadn't seen me, I hit the gas trying to get the heck out of there as tears stung the backs of my eyes.

Of course, I had to share my humiliation, so I called Krystal.

"I'm officially a stalker," I muttered, putting my phone on speaker. "And a bad one at that."

"Why? What happened?"

"I haven't heard from Drake since after the break-in, so I've been driving by the garage every night after I get off work wanting to catch him so we could talk," I explained with several sniffs.

"Oh, honey, you're okay. That makes perfect sense to me," she consoled. "We've all done it."

"But t-tonight, he was outside talking to Chanel," I said, dragging the last syllable of her name into about five as my tears caught up with me.

"That bitch," Krystal snapped. "Hey, come over! Mom brought me a casserole dish of her chicken enchiladas and I know you love 'em."

She didn't have to tell me twice because, yes, her mom made amazing enchiladas, but more importantly, I needed my best friend. "Okay," I replied with a snuffle. "Be there in ten."

I'd somewhat composed myself on the drive over, but when I walked into her apartment and she immediately gave me a big hug, I got all teary-eyed again.

"You go sit. I've already got your plate heating and I'll bring it to you," she said.

I plopped down on the sofa then looked at the TV to see that she had the movie *She's the Man*—one of my all-time favorites—paused and ready to roll just for me. Of course, this caused me to tear up again that she was such a good friend.

"What's wrong?" she asked, coming in and putting my plate on a trivet on her coffee table.

"You're s-such a g-good best friend," I choked out. "And I'm just a big bawl baby."

"Oh, honey," she said, sitting next to me and hugging me again. "It's all gonna be okay."

"I just don't understand why he won't open up to me. He's so closed off." I wiped under my eyes. "I don't understand."

"Like I said before, whatever he's hiding must be important to him, On. He asked for time, right?" I nodded. "If you want this to work, you have to give it to him."

"Pretty sure he's over it. I haven't heard from him all week," I pointed out.

"Then it'll be his loss, right?" she said softly, squeezing my hand.

I bit the inside of my lip and shrugged, hating her answer.

"You stop it right now, Honor Isadore Justice!"

I jerked my head back at her sudden chastisement since I'd expected compassion and not anger from her.

She kept going. "You are amazing. You're beautiful, smart, funny and you have an absolutely stellar career ahead of you. One you've chosen because you love helping people which means you're kind and caring! So stop this moping around." She looked me in the eye to make sure I was listening, which I was because you have to listen when someone uses your whole name. "I know you've had a lot going on what with Mr. Avery, Jeremiah and those assholes who roughed up Victor. But you need to suck it the hell up." Damn. She was definitely giving me the business. Then she threw out a real zinger. "And your happiness doesn't hinge on whether Drake Powers wants to be with you! I get that you care for him, but he's one guy in billions! If he's not all in with you, then...fuck him!"

I stared at her because I so needed to hear all that. And she was right. I'd been acting like a weepy, stupid mess instead of being strong.

"What's wrong with me?" I whispered.

She chuckled. "I want you to think back when Vic and I broke up. How did I act afterward?"

I thought for a second. "You cried. A lot." She nodded. "You were a mess for weeks."

"And what'd you tell me?"

I snorted. "I remember being so pissed and saying, 'Vic is a great big dumbass of a cunt if he thinks he can do better than you.' Then I told you how fabulous you are."

"Was I in love with him?"

"Yeah. You were," I said, nodding my head.

"So...does this mean you might be in love with Drake?"

My brow came down. "I don't know. I haven't really thought about it." I looked at my plate then gasped and turned to her. "Oh, God. I think I am."

She shrugged. "That's probably why you're so emotional then."

Huh. I was in love and didn't even know it. I guessed since I'd never been in love before, I hadn't known how it felt. "That explains why I've completely fallen apart." I looked at her. "Well, if this is being in love, it sucks ass," I murmured.

She giggled as she smoothed a few pieces of hair back behind my ear. "You're gonna be fine."

I looked at my best friend, giving her a sad smile. "I wish I'd known how it feels so I could've been nicer to you when you and Vic broke up."

"Water under the bridge. Now, let's get this movie started. I know you love how funny Amanda Bynes is and getting to look at Channing Tatum is just a huge bonus!"

Being with Krystal turned out to be just what I needed. The enchiladas were, of course, delicious and the movie had us both laughing even though we'd seen it a hundred times before.

~*~*~*~*~

By Friday, when I still hadn't heard from Drake, I'd finally come to accept that we were over.

And I was kind of okay with it. I mean, what other choice did I have. But Krystal had been right. Whether I was happy or not was all on me and not based on if I was with him. So I sucked it up and decided to move forward.

But one good thing had happened during the week. Before I left her house after our enchilada-slash-movie fest, Krystal told me she'd called Victor Monday after the break-in, like she'd said she would, and they'd been texting and talking all week. I was so excited, I broke my code of silence and jumped up and down doing baby claps as I squealed. I told her I'd wondered why Vic had been in such a good mood despite being accused of taking money from the bar and having a black eye.

Now as I walked into the house, home from work, my phone rang. I stupidly held out hope that it was Drake, but looking at the screen, saw it was my brother.

"Hey," I answered.

"Guess what?"

"What?"

"It *was* Ingram who was taking the money! The cops just left here with him in cuffs and he was singing like a fucking canary, telling everyone who'd listen that it was *Albert Mitchell* who hired him to steal the money. How fucking awesome is that?" He chuckled.

"Oh, my God. I can't believe Albert would do this."

"Yep. I heard he and Mom split up a couple months ago, and that she's already seeing someone else. I think he's pissed she moved on so fast and that's what prompted him to try to come after us."

"Wow." That was a lot of information packed in those two sentences. Jeez.

"I know. But I'm in the clear and Ingram's gone."

"I'm so glad they know it wasn't you. How'd they find out it was him?" I questioned.

"Dumbfuck used different employee IDs when he'd open the register to take money. When Finch started checking when money had gone missing, there were several times the person whose ID Ingram used wasn't even working that night."

"Good lord."

He laughed. "Yeah. And they're gonna pick up Albert tonight probably for burglary in the first degree, which Finch said is a class A felony so he's gonna get jail time. Oh, also conspiracy to commit a burglary. He's gonna lose his law license and be disbarred."

"Dang. This is all craziness," I said still trying to wrap my head around Albert trying to set up Vic, having held on to his anger for years now.

"Stupid crazy. Oh, and tomorrow, I'm taking Krystal to dinner—"

"Yay!" I yelled interrupting him. "I knew you'd finally come to your senses!"

He snorted. "'Bout time, huh? But we'd like to talk to you before we go."

"About?" I inquired.

"We both think it's time you knew why we broke up."

"Oh," I replied, somewhat shocked.

This was huge.

"Think you could be at the house tomorrow around four?" he asked.

"I can."

"Good. All right, just thought you'd wanna know what happened to Albert, which is fuckin' awesome!" He let out a whoop.

"It is!" I agreed, laughing. Not that I wished ill will on anyone, but Albert had so had this coming.

"Gotta go. I'll see you tomorrow, On. Love you," he said and hung up.

I showered then putting on sleep pants and a sweatshirt over my tank top, went to the kitchen and made snickerdoodles just because. Then after eating half a bowl of leftover vegetable soup, I went to bed, checking my phone to make sure I hadn't missed a call or a text.

I hadn't.

CHAPTER 19

Saturday morning I did laundry and cleaned around the house, finding myself nervous at what Victor and Krystal would tell me. I mean, what if it was something stupid and I had to gripe them out for keeping it under wraps for two years?

By the time Vic woke up and came into the kitchen around noon, I'd scrubbed it top to bottom and in the meantime had almost driven myself nuts thinking about what they'd tell me.

"Hey," he said, coming in and looking around for something to eat.

"Want me to heat you up some soup?" I asked.

"Sounds good," he said, getting a beer from the fridge then pulling out a chair and sitting.

As I ladled the soup into a bowl, I said, "I'm too impatient, aren't I?"

He chuckled. "Why do you say that?"

"Because I've bugged you guys, well, Krys, for details since you guys broke up." I put his bowl into the microwave and turned to look at him, leaning my butt against the counter.

He shrugged. "That's just curiosity."

"And I've driven Drake away now because he's held things back from me." I pushed off the counter and got him some saltines, placing the pack next to him.

"You guys broke up?"

"Pretty much," I shared, going back to get him a spoon. "Krys kept telling me to be patient and trust him, but I just wanted to know everything now." I set the spoon down next to him then went back to the microwave.

"You've always been that way, On. Like, since you were a fucking toddler. When you were three, you were on a mission until you found all our Christmas presents by digging through Mom and Dad's bedroom closet." He snorted.

The microwave beeped and I got his bowl out bringing it to him. "I did?"

"Yeah. That's how I learned there wasn't a Santa Claus. Thanks for that, by the way." He grinned as he crumbled crackers in his hands letting the crumbs fall into his bowl.

I sat down across from him. "See? My impatience ruins everything."

"Hey," he called making me look at him. "If a guy can't accept you the way you are then fuck him."

I frowned because that didn't help at all.

"On," he addressed me again. I raised my eyebrows at him. "You're the best person I know. And if he can't see that, then, seriously, fuck him."

Still not helping. I sighed.

"Want me to beat the shit outta him?"

I rolled my eyes. "Yes, because that would solve everything. No, my need to know everything ruined it. But I'll be fine. As Krys says, he's one in a billion guys and I don't need him to make me happy."

"She said that?"

I nodded. "She's pretty shrewd, Vic. You need to hold onto her this time."

"Damn. I better be on my game then if I'm just one in a billion who can only *try* making her happy." He grinned, cocky as ever, and I knew he wasn't the least bit afraid of the other nine hundred ninety-nine million nine hundred ninety-nine thousand nine hundred ninety-nine men out there.

"Remember, she deserves the best," I said before getting up. As I grabbed my brother some cookies from the jar, I commented, "So don't fuck it up."

"I'll try not to," he declared with a laugh.

"I'm going to the grocery store. Need me to pick you up anything?" I asked setting the snickerdoodles on the table.

"Yeah, shampoo, floss and shaving cream."

Grabbing my phone, I pulled up the notes and added his items to my list. "Got it. What time is Krys coming over again?"

"Around four."

"I'll be home in an hour which will give me enough time to make cherry cheesecake. Sound good?"

"Hell yes," he mumbled, holding the soup bowl up to his mouth and slurping the last of it down.

"Just make sure you don't do that at the restaurant tonight, or those other billion minus one guys might start looking good to Krys," I teased before leaving.

~*~*~*~*~

As I was checking out at the store, my phone rang. Great. Vic needed something else and I'd have to go back and get it.

I answered, not bothering to look at the screen. "What'd you forget?"

I heard a deep chuckle. Drake. Shit. "Not you." Yeah, right. We hadn't talked in days. He'd totally forgotten me. When I remained quiet, he asked, "Where are you?"

"Grocery store. Can I call you back?"

"I wanted to know if you had time to get a cup of coffee so we can talk?"

I looked at the time seeing it was just past one-thirty. "Sure. Where?"

He gave me the name and address of a little restaurant that I knew of and asked me to meet him there in an hour. We hung up and I finished checking out then loaded the bags into the back of Betsy, the whole time wondering what it could be he wanted to talk about.

On the way home, I called Krystal to see if she might have an idea but she didn't answer, so I was left to my own devices. But I must've channeled Krystal, because I told myself that whatever happened, happened, and I'd be fine no matter the outcome and I believed it. I might've loved Drake, but I knew I'd survive if things ended between us today.

Back at the house as I put everything away, Vic texted saying he'd gone to the gym the same time Krystal texted to let me know she was in a yoga class but would see me later and I had to chuckle at how in sync they were. I really hoped they worked out this time, but knew that if they didn't, they'd be okay too.

Wow. Look at me, all mature and enlightened. I was growing and that was a good thing. Krystal would've been proud of me right then.

I showered and got ready then went to meet Drake who was already at a table for two when I walked into the tiny place.

"Hey," he said, standing when he saw me approaching.

"Hi," I answered, wrapping my arms around his waist when he hugged me.

He drew back and looked down at me, his arms still around me. Smiling, he said, "Fucking sight for sore eyes, babe."

"You are too," I responded, giving him a small smile of my own then sat in the chair he pulled out for me. I ordered a soda when the waitress stopped at our table, seeing how he was drinking a beer. "Not really a coffee kind of day, huh?"

He chuckled. "No, I guess not."

We sat in what I felt was almost an uncomfortable silence waiting for the waitress to bring my drink. He was fidgety, messing with the salt and pepper shakers and I realized he was nervous.

When my drink came and the waitress left, I took a sip just as he said, "I love you, Honor."

Next stop, Choke City, of course.

"Wh-what?" I said between coughs, totally not what I thought he'd say.

He leaned over the table. "I said, I love you."

"Then why haven't I heard from you all week?" I blurted.

He sat back with a laugh. "You don't have to talk to someone all day every day to have feelings for them."

My brow came down. "I know that. But a text would've been nice."

He sighed. "Yeah."

Although it was thrilling to hear him say he loved me, I knew I couldn't say it back until I got some answers first. It'd been his idea to meet and I hoped he'd finally come clean and open up to me. If not, I didn't think there was much of a future for us. I took another sip waiting for him to go on.

Then he started talking. Thank God.

"Chanel pulls this shit every year. I just wanted to keep you out of it."

He paused as if waiting for me to say something but I wasn't about to interrupt him. I needed to know everything.

He let out a breath. "I told you I dropped out after my junior year when I got hurt in football." I nodded. "Being hurt wasn't the only reason. I quit to go to work." He took a drink. "Chanel and I started dating in the fall of our sophomore year." He scratched the side of his face looking a bit disconcerted. "The summer after our junior year, she got pregnant."

Oh, boy.

"We were going to get married and start our family together. We moved into the house I live in now and I thought everything was going great." He shrugged. "She hated being pregnant which made sense because she'd been modeling since she was sixteen and you know they have to look a certain way." He looked annoyed as he took a drink. "So we decided to wait to get married since she wanted to lose her baby weight to look perfect in her wedding dress. Nine months later, when my son Will was born on March twelfth, it was the happiest day of my life." The way his face lit up when he said that proved that it was his happiest day.

I'd figured Will might've been his son. As I mentally counted back to March twelfth, I found it explained the weekend he'd told me had been personal. It also told me Will had turned three. But why Drake had felt the need to hide all this from me, I didn't know.

He took another drink and continued. "After Will was born, Chanel withdrew. She didn't want to have anything to do with him. Or me, for that matter." He lifted a shoulder and let it drop. "Her mom has been out of the picture for the past ten years, so she didn't have anyone to help her. But my mom did all she could for her, helping with Will, talking with her, trying to get her to open up, babysitting so she could have time to herself. It just wasn't enough. Chanel said she missed modeling and wanted to travel. I told her we could make that happen, but nothing I came up with seemed to make her happy." He blew out a breath. "She finally told me she didn't love me and didn't want to marry me."

He held his beer mug up to the waitress who went to get him another. I sipped my soda staying silent not wanting him to stop talking.

After his beer came, he took a drink then said, "I have to tell you I was devastated. I loved her. I wanted to spend my life with her."

I nodded because of course he had. He was a good guy and I knew when he loved, he loved hard. I also knew Chanel was an idiot for letting him go.

"When Will was two months old, Chanel moved out and took off for Europe to model. I didn't hear from her for six months then she showed back up wanting to get back together. She moved back in that November and again we were happy I thought. But right after Will's first birthday she took off again saying she couldn't be with us, only to return six months later begging for another chance, which I foolishly gave. Right after Will turned two, she was gone again."

Well, shit. I knew he had trust issues because of something bad that'd happened but she'd pulled a frickin' doozy on him.

"Chanel's dad is a higher up at Amazon, travels a lot, kind of a playboy. He didn't have a lot to do with Will, I think he saw him twice, and he eventually ended up advising Chanel to sign over her parental rights. He pulled some strings with the court system and when Will was two and a half, I received the paperwork saying she'd terminated her rights. I guess the guilt got to her because she came back last September wanting to give it another go.

"I wasn't in love with her anymore, so I turned her down which pissed her off. She left the house and twenty minutes later, the police showed up and arrested me for domestic violence. I hadn't laid a fucking hand on her." The anger in his eyes was scary as he took another drink. "Thank God Mom was there when they arrived or they'd have taken Will and who knows where he'd have ended up. They cuffed me and took me in, fingerprinted me, mug shot, all that shit. Bad thing was, it was the Friday before Labor Day, so I spent the fucking weekend *and* Monday in jail waiting to go before the judge.

"I had to hire an attorney to try to prove I hadn't done anything to her. Of course, her dad has a shit ton of money, so she had her lawyers doing everything they could to drag things out, and other attorneys trying to get back her parental rights."

Good lord. She'd definitely put him through the wringer. I chewed the inside of my lip and reached a hand out to his, squeezing it then letting it go. "I'm so sorry, Drake."

He nodded slowly raising his eyebrows as if to say he was as well for ever being involved with her. "The case went to trial January of this year, and cost me almost twenty grand with court costs and attorney fees. The best part of it all was that once the trial started, the judge threw it out for lack of evidence, thank God. Of course, during all that time, Chanel was in and out of the country, living it up, not once asking to see Will. When her lawyers filed to get her parental rights back, she was turned down."

"Wow," I murmured.

Chanel had destroyed his faith in people. And even though I understood where he was coming from, still, it hurt my feelings that it seemed as if he'd lumped me in with her as not being trustworthy. Especially after getting to know me.

He now took my hand and held it, looking me in the eye. "So I hope you can see she's dangerous and why I have to be careful. There's no telling what she's capable of or to what extent she'd go if she knew I was seeing you, so I had to protect you. Since she came back about three weeks ago, she's threatened me nonstop, telling me she's going to find something she can hold against me and get Will back. That night when Jeremiah was parked down the street? Just as he took off another car did too and I found out she was having me fucking followed."

"Damn," I muttered.

"So I have to be careful of who I let into Will's life because she'd have her people do a background check and if anything questionable showed up, she'd sue me for custody or whatever else she could. Does that make sense?" he asked.

I narrowed my eyes wondering what she could find out about me, which I figured was next to nothing.

"I had to tell her when we were at the restaurant that you were just a customer who had a thing for me." He squeezed my hand hurrying to say, "I just didn't want to drag you into the thick of it." He next pulled me by my hand making me lean across the table where he too leaned in and brushed his lips against mine. "And I had to be sure you were someone I could trust."

I sat back, taking my hand from his and stared at him for a moment. "That's a lot to take in, Drake."

"I agree."

"So when she shows up, you pretty much have to do whatever she says because you're afraid she'll press imaginary charges against you and whatever else to try to get Will."

"Exactly."

"And I couldn't come to your house because her spies were watching you," I said.

"Yes. I didn't want her to use it against me. She could say I had women staying over which was bad for Will, even though it would've only been you."

Huh. I stared at him for a moment. "What were you arguing about in the parking lot that morning?"

"I usually let her see Will when she's back, which I did, but she wanted more time even though she had him all day for two days."

"Is it supervised?"

"Fuck yes. I wouldn't put it past her to hop on a plane and take him where I'd never find him."

That *would* be terrifying. But I was still a bit unsettled. "And you told her I was just an infatuated customer," I said.

I saw the sides of his jaws tic and he swallowed before answering. "Well, yeah. I had to protect you. She would've had her people dig into who you are."

"Why're you telling me all this now?" I asked.

"She left last night to go back to Milan."

Okay. Now I was mad. Not so much about his portraying me as a stalker. I got that, kind of. And it was more than understandable that he wanted to protect his child. That was a given. I also knew he was justified in not fully trusting someone with the way she'd screwed him around. But I felt as if I'd shown him exactly who I was and that he had nothing to worry about. So for him to keep this all from me really pissed me off.

"I appreciate your telling me everything. And while I understand you have to protect your son, what I don't get is that you're letting this woman dictate your life."

"Honor—" he interrupted.

"Let me finish," I said, raising my eyebrows asking for permission. When he conceded by breathing in through his nose and letting it out, I went on. "The fact that you felt you couldn't trust me with any of this hurts. If you'd just told me, I would've understood like I do now. And it's like you went behind my back with her, especially when you took her to the restaurant. If I'd known, it wouldn't have been that big of a deal." I held up a hand when he started to protest. "I can't pretend to act like I fully understand it all and how threatened you must feel, Drake. But telling her I was some infatuated customer, well, that's just unacceptable."

When I stood to go, he got out of his chair too.

"Honor, you have to understand, there's been no one in my life since her, until you. So this is all new to me. I handled it all wrong. I know that now." I nodded in agreement because yeah, he did. "But I love you and don't want to lose you."

I bit my bottom lip. "I love you too, Drake. But *I* need some time now," I whispered before walking out.

CHAPTER 20

When I got home from meeting Drake, I barely had time to make the cheesecake but I got it done. As I pulled it from the oven, Krystal came in.

"Hey! Oh, that looks delicious!" When I turned to her, she frowned. "What's wrong?"

"You look beautiful," I said, loving the stunning hot pink dress she wore that was sleeveless and in a racerback cut, the front coming up to her neck almost choker-style and spattered with white, sparkly crystals. "The cheesecake won't be ready until after you guys get back from your date," I explained.

"That's not what's bothering you."

"No, it's not." We sat at the table and I gave her a rundown about what Drake had said as she listened carefully.

"Well...I totally understand his side. But I absolutely get yours too," she declared. "Some help I am, huh?"

"I'm just gonna have to do some thinking," I said.

"You are. But he's right, On. He said he's never been in the situation of dating someone else with Runwayzilla in the picture, so I think you need to cut him some slack," she suggested.

"My brain is on overload," I confessed. "So now would probably be a good time for you and Vic to fill me in on everything." She laughed at my sardonic remark.

"Speaking of," she stated then called, "Victor! Are you ready?"

My brother walked into the kitchen looking sharp as hell in dark jeans, a charcoal gray blazer with a white button-up underneath and black lace-up boots.

"Damn, Vic!" I crowed upon seeing him. "You clean up nicely!"

He smiled at me but only had eyes for Krystal and that dress of hers murmuring a, "Fuck me."

"You like?" she said, spinning and smiling huge.

"I do," he answered. "You look beautiful."

"Thank you. You look pretty amazing yourself," she declared with a wink. She looked at me then back at him. "Are you ready to talk?" When he and I both replied in the affirmative, she asked, "Kitchen or living room?"

"Kitchen," I stipulated knowing I'd be more comfortable there.

I sat across from them and when Krystal looked at my brother, he nodded for her to start.

She took a deep breath and blew it out nervously then reaching across the table took my hand. "You know Victor and I started dating in October freshman year." I nodded. "You know I don't sleep around, but we," she looked at Vic, "fell pretty hard for each other and by November we were sleeping together." She looked back at me and smiled sadly. "Even though we were safe, I found out the next July that I was pregnant."

My mouth dropped open upon hearing that.

"We'd love to tell you there's a happy ending," Vic added. "But we lost the baby in August just before you two went back to school."

I glanced at them through the tears that had welled up in my eyes. "I'm so sorry."

Krystal brushed away a tear of her own that streamed down her face. "I'm sorry I didn't tell you, On, but we were both just shocked." She looked at Vic who put his arm behind her chair curling his hand around her shoulder. "After I miscarried we both felt guilty at being relieved about it since neither of us was ready for a baby."

"It began to build a wall between us so we decided that we should take a break," Vic said. He looked remorsefully at Krystal. "Then I screwed everything up. I was scared and ended up pushing you away."

Krystal sniffed as she looked at him, nothing but compassion in her expression. "I understood because it scared me too." She turned to me. "We didn't tell anyone. There were so many times I wanted to tell you, but when I'd start to, all the bad feelings would hit me again and I just couldn't."

"I understand," I told her dabbing at my eyes with a napkin.

"Missed the fuck out of you," Vic told Krystal. "I just didn't know then how to get to the place I'm at now."

"I know," she whispered with a hitch in her voice. "I was the same."

I was so sad that they'd been torn apart and even sadder that I could've had a niece or nephew who'd be two years old now. "I don't know what to say except I'm sorry," I told them. The doorbell rang and Vic moved to get up. "No, you stay with Krys," I said standing and going into the living room. Checking out the front window, I didn't recognize the guy on the porch. Upon opening the door, I saw he held a huge bouquet of flowers.

"Honor Justice?" he called through the storm door.

I frowned and nodded then opening the door took the arrangement from him. "Thank you," I whispered, staring at the gorgeous grouping of roses, tulips, daisies and what I thought was hyacinths. "Oh! Hang on," I told him, letting the storm door close before going back into the kitchen.

"Wow!" Krystal said when I walked in. "Are those from Drake?"

"I don't know," I replied, chewing the inside of my lip, just as surprised as she was, and, of course, secretly hoping they were from him.

I set the vase in the center of the table then went to the counter and grabbed a five from my wallet to tip the delivery guy.

Coming back into the kitchen, I saw Krystal and Vic standing embracing each other which made my heart glad. I walked over to the bouquet and sniffed. "They smell so good."

"They're beautiful," Krystal turned and said.

I pulled the card from its holder and opened it then looking at her nodded and whispered, "Drake."

"Yes!" she squealed. "He loves you!"

I rolled my eyes when she giggled but then giggled right along with her. She left Vic and gave me a hug. "It's all gonna be okay," she whispered.

"Thank you for always being here for me," I whispered back.

"Ditto," she said pulling back and smiling.

"Well, we're gonna take off before you two get any mushier," Vic said.

I looked at Krystal. "He's worried the estrogen level in here will affect his testosterone posibly making him human." She and I laughed together at the look he gave me. "I love you guys. Thank you for telling me everything."

"We love you too," Vic said, helping Krystal with her coat.

"Have fun tonight," I told them.

After they left, I stood in the kitchen staring down at the card.

I trust you implicitly.

Let me be your good guy, Honor—

I love you,

Drake

It was perfect and said everything I needed to hear.

But I was still hurt and needed more time to think on things, like maybe the fact that he had a crazy ex. If I stayed with him, could I deal with it when she pulled her shit again? Would he stand up for me or continue to pass me off as an infatuated customer? Would he expect me to disappear when she did come around?

Also, and more importantly, Drake had a son. Was I ready for that huge responsibility? Could I even handle having an instant family?

So much to consider.

I didn't call him that night to thank him for the flowers or to talk about any of the aforementioned. I would. Just not then.

Instead, I showered then threw on my U-Dub hoodie over my tank top and pulled on some sleep pants. In the kitchen, I emptied a can of cherries on top of the cheesecake and cut myself a piece. Then, since my brain was tired and I just needed to veg, I went into the living room and marathon-watched *The Office* on Netflix.

I laughed aloud several times at the crazy show, especially at Michael, Dwight and Andy's attempts at Parkour, before falling asleep on the couch with a rose in my hand I'd taken from the vase.

CHAPTER 21

Sunday morning I awoke in my bed not knowing how I got there. Then feeling warmth at my back, I turned over to see Krystal asleep next to me.

"You get drool on my pillowcase and you're washing it," I mumbled watching her eyelids flutter open.

"I put you to bed, Megara," she said in her raspy, just-waking-up voice. "You were so zonked I could've drawn a Sharpie mustache on you and you wouldn't have known it, so you'd better be nice to me."

"Think I was in a cheesecake sugar coma, Aurora," I responded with a yawn. "How'd last night go?"

She rolled to her back and stretched her arms up toward the ceiling letting out a squealy groan. "It was great." Turning her head toward me she shared, "It was like we'd never been apart."

"Good."

"I missed him."

"He's missed you."

There was a knock at the door and Vic called, "Is it safe to come in?"

"Only if you can handle all the gorgeousness going on in here," I hollered back.

The door opened and my brother strode in, first giving me a wink then his eyes went all soft when they landed on Krystal. "Hey, baby."

"Hi, honey," she said, reaching a hand out and pulling him to sit on the bed.

"Anyone want pancakes?" I asked, getting up and stretching before heading to the bathroom.

Two shouted "I do's!" followed me down the hallway.

~*~*~*~*~

After breakfast and cleaning up the kitchen, Krystal and I sat in the living room talking.

"So what're you gonna do?" she asked.

"I don't know. I'm still really hurt that he didn't trust me enough to fill me in on everything."

"I know you are. But you understand why he didn't, right?"

"Yes. But still..."

"You gonna come with us?" Vic asked, coming into the living room dressed to play football with the guys.

I made a face. "Eh. Probably not."

Krystal frowned. "You could talk to Drake afterward."

"I don't know," I said. "I still need to—"

The doorbell rang and I frowned getting up to see who it was. A small boy who was the spitting image of Drake—he was even dressed in jeans and a blue plaid shirt over a white t-shirt—stood on the porch with his big honey eyes looking up at me.

I opened the door and said, "Well, hey there."

He put his hands into his front jeans pockets looking shy and asked, "Aw you Awn-ah?"

Oh. My. Gosh. How freaking cute was that?

I smiled, squatting down in front of him. "Yes, I'm Honor. And what's your name, cutie?"

He grinned. "I'm Will!" he said proudly.

"Well, it's very nice to meet you, Will," I shared, grinning back at him.

Drake stepped out from where'd he stood at the side of the door. "Hey."

He looked so nervous as he gazed at me for a moment before bending down to pick up Will.

"Hey," I answered as I stood.

"Daddy," Will whispered, but in that kid whisper that's usually pretty loud and I chuckled.

"Yeah, buddy?" Drake mock-whispered back which made my heart melt a little.

Will put his mouth to Drake's ear, still "whispering." "She *is* pwetty like you said!"

Drake laughed as he looked at me. "I think the jig is up." Then he turned back to Will and said, "Yes, she is." He kissed the side of Will's head and I loved that he wasn't afraid to show affection to his son.

"Come on in," I told them.

Drake lifted his chin at Vic when he came in, saying, "Hey, man." He nodded his greeting at Krystal as Will started squirming, so he let him down.

"What's up?" Vic replied. Noticing Drake was dressed similarly to Will, he asked, "Not playing today?"

Drake glanced at me then back at Vic. "No. I've got more important things to do today."

"I wode in a big twuck!" Will told Krystal and Vic.

"You did? That's awesome!" Krystal declared at the same time Vic said, "That's pretty cool!"

I watched as Krystal took Vic's hand and they both looked at Will almost wistfully, and I knew they were thinking of the child they'd lost. Then she gazed up at my brother with a smile which he returned, both looking as if maybe Will had given them hope.

"We're gonna head out," my brother said. "Good seeing you, man." He nodded at Drake. Then he bent down getting eye-level with Will. "I'll see you later, okay, buddy?" He held his hand up and Will gave him a high-five.

After they left, I cocked my head to the side asking Will, "I'll bet you don't like cookies, do you?"

His eyes went wide and he nodded. "I wike cookies!"

"Well, why don't I get you some along with a glass of milk?" I looked at Drake to make sure it was okay, thinking I probably should've asked him first. Whoops.

Drake chuckled. "You give him cookies, you've made a friend for life."

I smiled and winked at Will. "I'll be right back."

Drake was sitting on the couch and Will was on his knees on the floor when I came back. A small truck had appeared from somewhere and Will was "vrooming" it across the floor.

"Here you go, Will," I said, setting the plate and the small travel mug I'd filled with milk on the new coffee table.

"Thank you!" He vroomed the car to the table on his hands and knees and once there grabbed up a cookie cramming it into his mouth.

Cutting my eyes to Drake, I mumbled, "Eats like his dad," which got me a sexy smolder. Gah!

All right, cool your jets there, Honor. You're still figuring things out, I mentally reprimanded myself.

Looking back at Will, I teased, "You probably don't like cartoons either, do you?"

He glanced at me like I was nuts looking so much like Drake it made me giggle as I got the remote and turned the TV on to a children's station.

"Is this one okay?"

"Yeah!" he answered, throwing a fist up into the air and he was good to go.

Putting my knee to the couch I sat and faced Drake. "He's adorable." My eyes went to Will, watching as he gobbled down another cookie, then I looked back at Drake. "And thank you for the flowers. They're beautiful."

"I'm glad you liked them." He sighed reaching out to take my hand. "I'm sorry about everything, babe. I've done a lot of thinking and I should've trusted you."

I shook my head gazing again at Will and stated, "I understand."

"I meant what I said on the card." I turned back to him. "I trust you. And I want you in my life. I love you, Honor."

Wow. He was saying all this in front of his son, who was busy watching a cartoon, but still.

"I love you too, Drake," I returned and was surprised when he leaned over and brushed his lips to mine because, again, he did this in front of Will. I peeked over but saw he wasn't paying a lick of attention to us. Phew. "Can I ask you a question?"

"Yep."

"If we're together and she comes back," I was careful not to mention Chanel's name in front of Will, "would I still just be an infatuated customer?"

Drake shook his head. "No. If you're in our lives, I wouldn't do that to you."

"I want to be in your lives...but the thought of becoming an instant mother figure scares the hell out of me."

"I get that. But, babe, you have to realize, he's never had that."

"What if I'm terrible at it?" I whispered. "What if I accidentally put a red sock in with the whites and turn all his underwear pink and he freaks out?"

He chuckled. "Babe."

My eyes got big when I mentioned, "Or I cuss and he learns bad words?"

Drake threw his head back as he barked out a laugh. When he finished chuckling, his eyes still sparkled with humor as he pointed out, "Honor. He has four uncles and a dad who curse like sailors, not to mention his grandpa, great-uncle and cousins. Believe me, you're not gonna say anything he hasn't already heard. I mean, of course, we try to watch our mouths around him, but sh—it happens. See?" He grinned.

I chewed the inside of my lip as I wrung my hands in worry. "I didn't have the greatest role model either, you know."

God. I really didn't want to screw up his precious son.

I felt a small body against my arm and turned to see Will standing there. He reached out and pulled my hands apart then climbed up into my lap resting his back against my chest.

As he snuggled in, he reached a hand up behind him and cupped the side of my face. "You're soft," he said with a yawn, his little fingers stroking my cheek, "you're" coming out more as "you-wah" which was the cutest thing ever and I knew I was completely smitten with this little boy.

I wrapped my arms around him holding him close as his little arm dropped from my face. "And you're snug as a bug in a rug," I whispered against the top of his head then kissed it. I looked up at Drake. "Is he asleep?"

He nodded, his eyes soft on me.

And just like that, I knew I'd be okay.

Will had most definitely been the unlikely hero of the day. Because of him, I'd witnessed the look of hope in the faces of my brother and best friend. And now there he was cuddled up with me, fast asleep, having put his trust in me, somehow knowing I'd keep him safe. I suddenly felt I could do this. And even if I screwed up with him, as long as I did it with love, I knew we'd be fine.

"He trusts me," I whispered, glancing up at Drake.

"Just like his dad," he replied, his eyes telling me he was sorry it'd taken him so long to get there.

And with that, I forgave him knowing he'd only done what he had to protect his son. And, boy, did I absolutely know that Drake protected what was his even if he sometimes went about it the wrong way. So we were good and I finally felt I was ready to try this with him.

And all it took was a three-foot-tall, adorable child to ease everybody's fears.

Huh.

"Are you happy?" Drake asked when I glanced up at him.

I grinned and made sure to pop the *P* when I replied, "Yep."

And I was.

EPILOGUE

I haven't met a lot of people who've made me want to be a better person, not by anything they said or did but just by being who they were, but Honor was one of them.

From the moment I met her, she kind of pissed me off, but in a good way, if that makes any fucking sense. I could tell she was someone who didn't settle—not meaning she was a snob, just someone who wanted the best for herself—and I respected her for it, although at the beginning I wasn't quite that receptive. I was too angry at what was going on in my life to give a fuck about anything else, but the fact that I was so attracted to her optimistic personality—of course her heart-shaped ass and great tits also drew me in (I'm a guy, get over it)—irritated the hell out of me.

Although I tried keeping her away from the shit storm that was my life by being a total asshole to her, when I finally woke up to see the sweet, beautiful, selfless woman who was right in front of me, I stopped feeling sorry for myself and had to go for it.

Was it selfish? Probably. Did I care? Nope. I wanted her and I got her and that's all that fucking matters.

From the beginning, she's kept me on my toes, challenging me to be better, and not just for her and Will but also for me. The innocence she exudes makes me fall in love with her more every day in the way she tries living her life the best way she knows how.

As for the secrets I kept from her, although I understood her frustration, I just didn't know how to have the girl yet keep her safe at the same time. Thank God she gave me a chance to make things right or I'd be back to being the miserable bastard I was when we first met.

She says she's too impatient, that she wants to know things right now so she can be prepared for what else is coming or find a way to fix things. I think it's cute that she's so antsy and it's what makes her who she is.

I went through hell on the way to finding her. The fact that she wants to stick around and be by my side during not only the good times but also the bad just makes me love her that much more.

I once told her I wasn't the good guy she was looking for.

But, by God, I'll try every day for the rest of our lives to be him.

Just for her.

Sneak peek at Rock the Dream (Redfall Dream #1) by B.B. Miller and Leslie Carson coming up!!

ABOUT THE AUTHOR

USA Today Best Selling author Harper Bentley writes about hot alpha males who love hard. She's taught high school English for 24 years, and although she's managed to maintain her sanity regardless of her career choice, jumping into the world of publishing her own books goes to show that she might be closer to the ledge than was previously thought.

After traveling the nation in her younger years as a military brat, having lived in Alaska, Washington State and California, she now resides in Oklahoma with her teenage daughter, two dogs and one cat, happily writing stories that she hopes her readers will enjoy.

You can contact her at harperbentleywrites@gmail.com, at harperbentleywrites.com, on Facebook or on Twitter @HarperBentley

Check out other titles by Harper Bentley:

The Powers That Be series:

Gable (The Powers That Be Book 1)

Zeke (The Powers That Be Book 2)

Loch (The Powers That Be Book 3)

Ryker (The Powers That Be Book 4)

CEP series:

Being Chased (CEP #1)

Unbreakable Hearts (CEP #2)

Under the Gun (CEP #3)

The High Rise series

The Fighter

Serenity Point series:

Bigger Than the Sky (Serenity Point Book 1)

Always and Forever (Serenity Point Book 2)

True Love series:

Discovering Us (True Love #1)

Finding Us (True Love #2)

Finally Us (True Love Book 3)

True Love: The Trilogy: The Complete Boxed Set

The Wait series:

Thursdays (The Wait Book 1)

http://harperbentleywrites.com/

ROCK THE DREAM

Chapter 1

Kennedy

"DON'T YOU WANT more?" My voice sounds disembodied, dry, and raspy, like I'm a seventy-five-year-old chain smoker who doesn't give a shit about what a lifetime of nicotine has done to his lungs.

A booming bass fills the penthouse suite at the San Francisco Fairmont, where my band, Redfall, and a host of strangers party into the night. "Mmm... You're so fucking hot." It's a slurred and intoxicated whisper against my neck from some nameless groupie sitting on my lap. Gin and desperation roll off her in waves. She licks the curved chaos of ink snaking down my shoulder and grinds her skinny, naked body against mine. I shudder at the feel of skin and bones against me. She pushes her tits forward, and breathes in my ear. "Touch me, Kenny."

"I always want more. So do you." The voice of my tour manager, Brodie Dixon, drifts to me from somewhere far away. I lean back against the couch, trying to open my eyes in an attempt to find him. I feel like I'm floating in a dream or a nightmare; it's hard to tell which. I'm stuck somewhere between reality and a fucked up fantasy.

"Name's Kennedy," I mumble.

"Kenny, Kenny, Kenny," she chants as she rolls her hips against mine.

I turn my neck in the direction I think Brodie's voice came from, making a feeble attempt to brush away the hand flattening against my stomach, and drifting south. I can feel her jagged nails scratching over my hip, fumbling, as she attempts to unhook my leather belt.

Her hot, liquor-laced breath fans over my exposed chest, and her fingers lazily drift along the tatt that covers my neck. She doesn't give a shit about me. She's just here because I'm Kennedy-Fucking-Lane and she wants to say she fucked me.

Somehow, I manage to open my eyes. Through an intoxicated haze, I can make out Brodie—at least I think it's him—bent over a table, slowly moving his face along a mirrored surface. I lift the dead weight of the bottle of Jack to my lips, welcoming the burn as the whiskey hits my throat.

Muted light filters in from the gaps in the curtains, catching the glare from the mirror and splaying prisms of color over Brodie's body. He leans back in the chair and lifts his hand to his nose, snorting back any excess coke he may have missed. He cracks his neck like he always does when he's finished, and pats his thigh.

It feels like I'm watching in slow motion as a groupie appears like an apparition out of nowhere and floats to his lap, immediately wrapping her arms around his neck and crashing her lips to his.

I shut my eyes, guiding the heavy bottle back to my lips, hoping the magic liquid will block everything out. It hurts to swallow. My throat feels like it's on fire. I wonder how much is enough to numb the pain.

"No. I mean more than this," I say, setting the bottle back on the couch.

"I've got more right here, man." The unrelenting music pounds in my head, and I hear the sound of the chair scraping across the hardwood floor as the room spins.

Shuffled feet make their way across the room. I hear a crash, broken glass hitting the floor, and then a fit of giggling.

"I fell. Kiss it better, Brodie." That high-pitched voice is like nails on a goddamn chalkboard.

I open one eye to find Brodie leaning against me. "Mmm... You've got more, too, I see. What's your name, sugar?" Brodie gives a lazy grin to the blond perched in my lap.

"Whatever you want it to be," she says slowly, leaning forward to press her lips to my neck.

I try to roll my eyes, but it's too much work in my current fucked-up state. From the floor, the giggles continue and Brodie laughs, big and boisterous, reminding me I'm, in fact, still alive.

The girl on my lap rolls her head back, her bleached hair spilling against my jean-covered thighs. Pouring a stream of whiskey over her tits, my tongue lazily follows the trail. "Mmm... More, but not real. I miss real tits."

"They're tits, man—real, fake, what's the difference?"

"More... The difference is more."

Brodie leans over me and cups her breast in his hand. "Well, I like them, sweetheart. Come here."

It doesn't take much coaxing to pull her from my lap. She squeals while I try to make my escape, pushing off the cushions a few times to get somewhat vertical. The room sways, and I stumble back against the arm of the couch.

My vision blurs to the point I can only make out shapes—changing, shifting, and morphing shapes that seem to deliberately block my path.

I take in the bodies currently grinding together in an erotic, tempting dance. They're everywhere and nowhere at the same time. Against walls, windows, furniture, molded to the floor. It's like a fucking funhouse in here.

"I'm just gonna..." The world tilts, and my eyes slide shut.

"You're high as a motherfucking kite, Lane," Brodie yells from the couch.

My grip tightens around the neck of the bottle as I step over a pair of endless long legs pushed into high-heeled fuck-me boots. I register something slicing into my foot, and I welcome the pain.

I stumble to the black grand piano where there's a couple of plastic bags open, their powdery contents spilling out. I can almost hear them calling my name.

Somewhere in all the haze and drug-induced madness of my currently fucked-up, fried brain I know if I take another drink or do another line, it may be my last. The scary part is that somewhere in there I kind of want it to be.

Through my blurry vision, I see a solid mass of muscle standing ready in the hall. I think it's Tucker Pearson, my security guard, and one of the only real friends I have left. He shakes his head in my direction, and makes the decision for me.

Leaving Brodie and the rest of my band to the squealing groupies, I shuffle my way to the first door I find, push it open, and welcome the softness of the bed as I collapse face first into it.

Welcome to the life of a motherfucking rock star.

ଓଃ

"Get up, asshole."

I groan from a tangle of covers and pillows. Maybe Tucker will go away if I just lay here. It hurts too much to move anyway. The warm covers fly off me, exposing my bare back to the assault of the cool air conditioning.

"Fuck, man. Give me a second."

He opens the blinds to the terrace, and I blink at the harsh sun streaming in. My head pounds and I burrow my face into the pillow, waiting for the welcome darkness to descend. I made it to another day. Halle-fucking-lujah.

"You look like shit."

He grips my hair, forcing my head back as I fight to open my eyes. Even in my fucked-up state, I can see the disappointment in his face. He shakes his head and tightens his hand in my hair.

"Is this what you want, huh? This is what you worked so hard for?"

"Fuck off, Tucker."

"You've got the meeting with the charity today. Did you forget about that? The dream for the sick little boy?"

"Mmm..." It hurts when I try to shake my head. "T'morrow."

I try to push him away. It's almost impossible at the best of times, given Tucker's sheer size and strength let alone trying it after a night like the one I just survived.

"It *is* tomorrow, idiot."

He pushes my head forcefully into the pillow. The bed dips with his weight. "This has got to stop, man. You want to be *that* cliché? Musical genius who drank and snorted himself into oblivion?"

"What I don't want is a lecture from you right now." My voice is muffled against the pillow.

"You're better than this, Kennedy." His voice is quieter, and I manage to turn my head in his direction, opening my eyes.

"Not anymore."

"You are. Why don't you let me check out that rehab place? The one in Malibu?" It's not the first time he's suggested it.

"Right, 'cause that's not a cliché at all, is it?"

"They deal with celebrities all the time. They have confidentiality rules and—"

"And what? You want me to sit and talk about my goddamn feelings like the last time I tried rehab? That's bullshit, man." I wince as the jackhammer rattles in my head. "Fuck, where's the goddamn Oxy?"

He moves from my vision, and I close my eyes, welcoming the quiet. I stretch my arm out beside me, my hand making impact with warm skin. The room spins as I turn my head, glancing over at the body beside me. I think she might be the giggler from the floor last night, but I'm not sure.

"Shit." I manage to push myself up and lean back against the plush headboard. I don't want to see her half-naked body draped over the rumpled bed. At least I still have my jeans on. Little victories amuse me, and I try to laugh, but it hurts too much.

My stomach rolls as she lets out a moan, lifting her head just off the pillow, her eyes glassy and unfocused as she stares blankly at me. "Ready again so soon, handsome?"

In the cruel, harsh light of the morning after, everything is different. Here I am, in a lush penthouse suite with a strung-out junkie, whose name I don't even want to know beside me.

The raccoon eyes are in full force as she clumsily wipes them, leaving more mascara smudged beneath her lashes. "I just need a little something first. Got any smack?" She tries to push herself up, but doesn't seem to have the strength. She dissolves back to the bed with a giggle.

I close my eyes and swallow down the razor blades lining my throat.

"Tucker?" I strain to hear him moving around in the bathroom. I think I doze off right there, leaning up against the headboard with my head feeling like a tire iron has been rammed through it, until ice-cold water splashes down over me.

"Jesus, fuck!" My body convulses when I try to push off the bed. I glare at Tucker as he holds an empty ice bucket. The giggler squeals louder in hysterics.

"You—in the shower. Now." He scowls at me, daring me to defy him.

The frigid water drips from my damp hair as I push off the soaked bed. He shakes his head, his lips curling up into a knowing smile. I think Tucker's patience is running out, but for now, I know I'm forgiven for another night of debauchery.

"Do something with that, will you?" I tilt my head in the direction of the giggler. He knows the routine. Wipe her phone, pay her well, and remind her of the confidentiality agreement she no doubt has forgotten she signed when she was sober.

"I'm on it," he replies, while I drag my sorry ass to the bathroom. I curse as pain shoots through my foot, and I struggle to remember what happened last night.

It's not unusual for me to have blackouts where I have absolutely no idea what I did or how I got to be in the place I wake up in. I know I'm existing on a very thin and unstable line. I've been looking to the bottle to fill up a gaping hole in me. If left unchecked... the siren call to make the pain go away is too strong for me to resist.

It's one of the reasons I'm grateful for Tucker. He's the one who pulls me back to reality after a night of excess. Why he hasn't left me is a miracle. But he's here, dealing with what I can't. I can hear shouting from the giggler behind the closed door while he cleans up my mess one more time.

Leaning against the cool marble vanity, I squint in the harsh lighting. I hardly recognize the gaunt face staring back at me. Fumbling with the tap, which is harder to figure out than it should be, I finally get the cold water to turn on. I lean over the basin and splash water on my face.

I hate myself for admitting that Tucker is right. I'm getting too old for this shit. You could easily mistake me for an addict on the street instead of a successful musician who should be on top of the world.

Under the glare and buzz of the fluorescent lights in the luxury of the bathroom bigger than my first apartment, it dawns on me: I've just used the word I have always refused to associate with myself. *Addict.*

The bathroom door opens, and Tucker steps into view in the mirror beside me. He's the picture of health and life. A sharp contrast to what I'm becoming.

"What are you doing? If she was here, if she could see you—"

I meet his eyes in the mirror. "Don't go there, man. Just don't."

"I have to."

I glare back at him. "If I piss you off this much, why the fuck do you stick around?"

"You know damn well why. I promised Rob—"

"Don't. Don't you dare say her name." I clench my teeth, feeling my jaw set.

He glares at me in disgust. "Do you think this is what she would've wanted for you?"

We stare at each other in the mirror in a silent standoff, neither one of us wavering.

"Oxy is beside the sink. Drink this." He tosses me an energy drink—some pink colored shit that tastes like hell, no doubt. "All of it. Shave the forest you've got growing on your face, and take whatever you need to appear somewhat alive and coherent. The charity team will be here at one."

My hands shake as I go for the pain meds. It's a fight to get the lid off. Finally, I pour a couple of pills into my wet palm and lift my gaze to meet his in the mirror.

"You're really living the dream, Lane. Living the dream."

ଔ

Abigail

"Got a minute, boss?"

My eyes pop up from the spreadsheet I've been struggling

with. Tessa Baker, my assistant, is poised at my doorway. Grateful

for the interruption, I smile.

"Sure. What's up?"

She strides into my office and hands me a sheaf of papers.

"We have the final report on the Peterson Dream."

"Oh, good. We really lucked out on that one." I still can't

believe we'd been able to fulfill ten-year-old Ryan Peterson's dream

of being with his beloved Seattle Seahawks when they won the

Super Bowl. The lucky part hadn't been sending Ryan to the game—

the Seahawks and NFL had been only cooperative. It was whether

Ryan's bone cancer, which had accelerated, would allow him to

attend. It had been a race against time.

I scan the report with my usual mixture of pride and sorrow;

pride because we were able to provide this for a spunky young boy

who sorely deserved it, and sorrow because he had lost his fight with

his illness only three weeks after the event. As the executive director

for *What's Your Dream*, I'm more than familiar with the emotions.

Although we'd only been in existence ten years, we'd already

fulfilled more than three thousand dreams of children with terminal or life-threatening illnesses. Since I'd become director three years ago, we'd doubled the number of chapters. Soon, we'll have one in every state.

"His parents were so grateful," Tessa comments, her eyes full of understanding.

I nod again, my brow furrowing as I recall his mother's voice when she'd called to let us know about Ryan's passing. I couldn't help but cry with her over the phone as she'd described his last days. How happy and thankful he'd been to not only attend the game with his family, but to also have the chance to hold the Lombardi trophy—with the help of a few of his favorite players. It had been all he'd talked about, right up until the end.

Moving the report aside, I take a settling breath and stand, smoothing my black pencil skirt. "Okay, then. Everyone waiting for me, I suppose?" I look at my assistant.

Tess ticks something off on her clipboard. "Just April, of course. But the others are on their way."

We leave my office and Tess follows me down to one of our smaller meeting rooms. April is seated at the table, texting someone. I swear, the girl was born with a phone in her hand.

"You're late." She doesn't look up.

Smirking, I take the seat opposite her. "Happens to the best of us once in a while, April," I quip as the rest of our group files in and take their places.

"Yeah, yeah," she retorts with a sigh, and places her phone on the table. She flips her glossy, straight black hair over her shoulder. April Morrison is our public relations director and damn good at her job. I'd managed to coax her away from Make-A-Wish last year, and I constantly thank my lucky stars. She's sharp, tireless, and loyal, and her penchant for punctuality has become legendary.

"So, what do we have this week?" I open the folder in front of me and glance up to our giving director, Nadia Baskov, sitting next to April.

"Sixteen dreams were already approved by the Eligibility team this week"—she takes a sip of her tea—"but they bumped these seven cases up to us."

I hum in understanding. Although our Eligibility team is responsible for evaluating each request, they only implement the relatively straightforward dreams, such as those for new pets, birthday parties, or trips. The more complex requests are sent upstairs where the four of us—April, Nadia, Duane Allen, our finance director, and I—deliberate on the possibilities and appropriateness of the requests.

I skim through the seven cases before sitting back to let Nadia take us through each one. Her fingers toy absently with a lock of her silky blond hair. With her sharp green eyes and stylish navy suit, she looks the epitome of a cold, calculating businesswoman, but underneath her austere demeanor beats a sensitive and compassionate heart.

A twelve-year-old girl with a brain tumor wants an audition with the Moscow Ballet. Hmm, that's a little tricky in the current political climate. However, Nadia's cousin is a trainer with the San Francisco ballet… maybe that could work instead. A six-year-old boy from Colorado with a degenerative lung condition wants to score a goal against his favorite hockey star. A ten-year-old boy with MS loves airplanes and dreams of being a pilot; my contact at Alaska Airlines can provide a complete tour, everything from the tarmac to the cockpit. Maybe we can throw in a trip to one of the flight schools, too.

We work through the cases, discussing the merits of each and formulating initial plans. The children's faces that peer up at me from the folder look happy and hopeful, but when I read their stories... I glance out the large window at the bright blue sky, blinking back tears. I hate that so many virulent diseases threaten so many young lives. So many futures at risk. So many poems and symphonies to write, or planets and species to discover. One of the children we see here could hold the key to solving the world's greatest problems, but may never get the chance.

Ever since I was fifteen, when I saw what cancer could do, I've wanted to do something about it. Science has never been my forte, so I knew I wouldn't be the one who would find the cures. But I could do something to ease the patients' suffering and bring a little joy to their lives, as well as the lives of their families.

"You okay there, Abby?" I glance up to see April's concerned face. We all have our moments when the stories and the kids behind them break through the professional veneer we try to maintain during these meetings. Last week it was Tess who'd had to excuse herself during the discussion of a six-year-old boy with Non-Hodgkin's Lymphoma, who simply wanted to take his grandfather to

Disney World. The grandfather had been an illustrator for some of the Disney movies back in the sixties.

I suddenly become aware that I've brought the discussion to a halt. "Yes, I'm fine," I assure her and nod at Nadia. "You were saying?" I smile encouragingly, and she continues, holding the last profile aloft.

"Now, I think I sent to you the details on the meeting we're having today a few days ago, Abby, but I haven't heard your thoughts on it yet." Nadia fans the pages out on the table. She takes a breath and slowly lets it out, her eyes lingering the last page.

"This is Parker Jensen," she begins, indicating the grinning blond boy on the top sheet. "Eleven years old with leukemia. He lives right here in San Francisco, and his dream is to enjoy a day as a rock star with…" She taps the second photo in the set, and there is a collective intake of breath around the table.

"Oh, my," April says appreciatively. "He's aged well, hasn't he?"

"Kennedy Lane?" Duane questions. "Isn't he a little old for the preteen crowd?"

Nadia's eyeing the photo like it's a triple-decker hot fudge sundae. "He's not *that* old," she scoffs. "He's only thirty-six. Apparently, Parker idolizes him. He's learning to play the guitar and wants to be just like Lane when he grows up." Her expression becomes wistful. "And I hope he has the chance."

We're silent for a moment. The thought Parker may not get a chance to grow up sobers us. Then April sighs, a smirk curving her lips. "Well, Parker has excellent taste in music. I don't remember how many awards this guy has won, but he's incredible. And when you throw in that *face*..." She points to the publicity photo. "I think spending a day with Kennedy Lane would be my dream, too."

Tess giggles in agreement; Duane rolls his eyes at her. "Oh, please. Get over yourselves. You don't see Abby getting all swoony. Besides, when was Redfall's last hit? They're never on the radio anymore," he complains.

"Abby never gets swoony. And, Redfall has a new album coming out soon," April shoots back, peering at Duane over her chic cat-eye glasses.

"Oh, what? I suppose the money's running low, so he's going to squeeze out something to make the teenage girls and their mothers scream? Then he'll take his money and run back to wherever aging rock stars go when they retire?"

"What's got into you?" A frown mars Nadia's lovely features. "We deal with celebrities all the time."

He shrugs. "I just don't think he'd be a good influence, that's all. The kid should idolize someone more worthwhile."

"They can't *all* want to go to Disneyland." April waves her hand at him. "And Lane is more than a rock star; he's an artist. At least, he was."

Their sniping fades into the background as I peruse the two pages. Parker is adorable with bright blue eyes and an infectious grin. Lane is... Actually, I'm not sure what Lane is. Handsome seems inadequate when you consider his chiseled jawline and sensual pout. But, April is right; he's so much more than his looks. The complex rhythms and cerebral lyrics that have always characterized his sound set him apart from his contemporaries. His band was a staple during my college years and beyond; in fact, I have dozens of Redfall's songs on my playlists now.

But how wise would it be fulfill this particular dream? Parker's treatments have left him in a fragile state. Is Kennedy Lane the type of man who would understand—and respect—that?

I'd started researching him as soon as Nadia had sent me the report, but had come up with mixed results so far. His older interviews revealed an intelligent, whimsical mind that appealed to me. He sounded like someone I'd love to sit with for a beer and conversation. His more recent comments in the press, however, had sounded so angry. Arrogance and negligence had replaced the whimsy and playfulness. Maybe he succumbed to the pampered celebrity lifestyle, or maybe it was just a bad day. Who knew?

I flip the promo photograph over, focusing on the more recent paparazzi photos Nadia included in the packet. The photos captured him leaving a club with his entourage. He was obviously annoyed and probably drunk. But more than that, there was something in his eyes…something familiar in that glazed stare…

I manage to suppress a shudder when a particularly unpleasant memory leaps to mind; a memory of screamed threats, desperate begging, and a final, terrifying good-bye. My ex, Lucas, had hid his addiction before finally slipping up. After months of pleading and empty promises of rehab, his inability to change led me finally to wipe my hands clean of the mess his addiction had made of our lives.

It's funny how having a gun pressed to your temple can make everything so clear.

"Abby? What do you think?" My attention snaps back to the here and now, and I see all eyes trained on me. I take a deep breath to compose myself, and lock the past where it belongs—in the past.

"Actually, Duane has a good point." I ignore how he puffs up his chest at my comment. "I'm not sure if exposing a young boy to this *scene* is a good idea. You know, the whole sex, drugs, and rock 'n roll' thing." I hold up a hand when I see Nadia getting defensive. "I know—it's a stereotype. But, I'm honestly concerned why Lane dropped out of sight for so long. Was he in rehab? Or was he off on some spiritual journey meditating with the Dalai Lama or something?" I pause and thoughtfully tap the photos with my fingertips. "All that aside, granting wishes is our mission. If we can make this happen, we should. We'll have a better idea once we meet with his team today."

"*We?*" There's no mistaking the annoyance in Nadia's voice. "Well *I* have an appointment with his manager and a representative from his record label at the Fairmont at one. The record label was very enthusiastic."

"Will Lane be there, too?"

She adjusts her glasses, looking like the cat that got the cream. "There is that distinct possibility."

I share a quick glance with April; she cocks an eyebrow, and I know she's also noticed Nadia's odd demeanor.

"I'm going with you."

"Oh, uh…" She falters, drawing my gaze up to hers. Nadia rarely hesitates. "Are you sure? You don't usually attend these sorts of meetings, Abby."

"I know, but I want to ensure this goes smoothly." At her sharp look, I add, "I've heard Lane's manager can be difficult, and you might need the extra firepower." I don't want her to think I doubt her abilities. Nadia is extremely skilled at her job. I'm probably misreading her—she's too professional to fuck around with a case, literally *or* figuratively. "And, given what we've just discussed about the potential negative influences in his lifestyle, I'd like to hear for myself if his team understands Parker's situation."

She hums, sounding mollified, and peers at me speculatively. "This is one of those cases for you, isn't it?"

I sigh, knowing that she's right. Sometimes, a dream fulfillment will hit you just the right way, and it becomes "yours." And apparently Parker Jensen, with all his struggles and his soulful eyes that touch my heart, has become one of mine.

"I guess you're right."

"Okay," she replies, with a touch of resignation. "I'll send the appointment over to Tess so she can arrange your calendar."

Duane deflates with Nadia's statement, and we quickly adjourn. I exit the room, pretending not to hear Duane calling my name. I'm not in the mood for whatever he wants to say, especially if he's going to complain about my decision. I swear, the man can pout worse than a thirteen-year-old girl.

Back in my office, I tuck a stray hair back into my perfect chignon and adjust the collar of my crisp cotton blouse. Not bad for thirty-four, but still, April is right. 'Swoony' is definitely not a word I subscribe to, not even for fuckhot rock stars.

Sitting at my desk, I pull Lane's promo photo out of the file and stare at it. Peering out from beneath a mop of thick black hair, those deep blue eyes seem to leap off the page to see right through me. It's disquieting. Suddenly, the only word I can think of to describe Kennedy Lane is... *dangerous*... in more ways than one.

But how can I say no when he's a little boy's heart's desire?

Made in the USA
San Bernardino, CA
06 February 2019